SHOWDOWN

"Draw!" he yelled, and dropped his hand.

"This is for Anne," Brionne said, and for an instant Cotton Allard's hand froze.

Then his gun leaped up and he fired. Brionne felt the slug as a tremendous blow. It hit him, knocking him back through the door.

He came up to his knees, then to his feet. He lifted his gun as Cotton stepped into the door and fired again.

Brionne staggered. He had no doubt that Cotton would get him, but he intended to kill Allard first . . .

Bantam Books by Louis L'Amour

Ask your bookseller for the books you have missed

BENDIGO SHAFTER
BORDEN CHANTRY
BRIONNE
THE BROKEN GUN
THE BURNING HILLS
THE CALIFORNIOS
CALLAGHEN
CATLOW
CHANCY
COMSTOCK LODE
CONAGHER
DARK CANYON
DOWN THE LONG HILLS
THE EMPTY LAND
FAIR BLOWS THE WIND
FALLON
THE FERGUSON RIFLE
THE FIRST FAST DRAW
FLINT
GUNS OF THE TIMBER-
    LANDS
HANGING WOMAN
    CREEK
THE HIGH GRADERS
HIGH LONESOME
HOW THE WEST WAS
    WON
THE IRON MARSHAL
THE KEY-LOCK MAN
KID RODELO
KILLOE
KILRONE
KIOWA TRAIL
THE MAN CALLED
    NOON
THE MAN FROM
    SKIBBEREEN
MATAGORDA
THE MOUNTAIN
    VALLEY WAR
NORTH TO THE RAILS
OVER ON THE DRY SIDE
THE PROVING TRAIL

THE QUICK AND THE
    DEAD
RADIGAN
REILLY'S LUCK
THE RIDER OF LOST
    CREEK
RIVERS WEST
SHALAKO
SILVER CANYON
SITKA
THE STRONG SHALL LIVE
TAGGART
TUCKER
UNDER THE SWEET-
    WATER RIM
WAR PARTY
WESTWARD THE TIDE
WHERE THE LONG GRASS
    BLOWS
YONDERING

Sackett Titles by
Louis L'Amour

---

1. SACKETT'S LAND
2. TO THE FAR BLUE
    MOUNTAINS
3. THE DAYBREAKERS
4. SACKETT
5. LANDO
6. MOJAVE CROSSING
7. THE SACKETT
    BRAND
8. THE LONELY MEN
9. TREASURE
    MOUNTAIN
10. MUSTANG MAN
11. GALLOWAY
12. THE SKY-LINERS
13. THE MAN FROM THE
    BROKEN HILLS
14. RIDE THE DARK
    TRAIL
15. THE WARRIOR'S PATH
16. LONELY ON THE
    MOUNTAIN

Brionne

1

The night brought a soft wind. It came gently, flowing through the gaps in the Blue Ridge Mountains and spilling over the valleys below, rustling the leaves outside the big house. They rustled, were still, then again they stirred.

Mat Brionne, who was not quite seven, lay awake, listening.

His father was in Washington to see President Grant, but was expected home soon, and Mat was eager for any sound that might herald his coming.

Mat loved his father, a tall, fine-looking man in uniform or out, a superb horseman, and as the neighbors said, "as fine a shot as ever held a gun."

The rustling of leaves stilled momentarily, and in the silence Mat heard a faint stir of horses moving up the lane from the highroad. These horses moved almost silently, which was not like his father's coming would be.

The curtains at the window were open, and in the faint light Mat could see the hands of the clock. He had just learned to tell time, and was very aware of each hour. It was past midnight. As he listened, the sounds ceased. Uneasy, remembering the stories of Indians and of renegades, he slipped from his bed and peered down into the yard.

For a moment he saw nothing, and then he caught the shine of an empty saddle, then a surreptitious movement in the shadows near a tree.

Frightened, he went down the hall to his mother's room. He opened the door, went in quickly, and touched her arm.

"Mother . . . there's some men outside. I heard them."

"It's your imagination, Mat. Your father won't be back until tomorrow."

"I didn't think it was pa. They're acting very quiet. I'm scared."

Anne Brionne got up and took her robe from a chair. There had been no trouble to speak of in Virginia since the end of the war, when James had been rounding up renegades.

"It's alright, Mat. No one would come to bother us. They know your father too well. Anyway, Sam would have heard them. He's sleeping in the gate-house."

"Mother, this is Friday. Sam's never there on Friday. He goes to the tavern."

Nobody was supposed to know that, but Mat had overheard the overseer telling Sam to be careful—that if the Major heard about it he would be discharged.

Anne Brionne stood very still, thinking. The nearest house was four miles away. Burt Webster, their overseer, had gone to visit his sister in Culpeper. The field hands were cutting firewood back in the mountains, and if Sam was gone they were alone on the place, except for the Negro maid, Malvernia.

"There's nothing to be afraid of, Mat. We'll go downstairs."

Their feet made no sound upon the soft carpets. James kept his guns locked in a cabinet in his study, but when they reached the foot of the stairs Anne Brionne paused, facing the front door. Someone was trying the door, turning the knob ever so gently. Mat heard it, too, and his grip on his mother's hand tightened.

For a moment she stood perfectly still, and in that instant she felt fear for the first time. Suddenly she knew who the men must be—in Virginia, at this time, it could be nobody else. This was a time of peace. There had been little lawlessness since James ended the raids by the guerilla bands left over from the war.

Two years had gone by, but she still remembered the courtroom and the evil, hate-twisted face of Dave Allard as he hurled threats at her husband, Major James Brionne.

The Allards—it was a name they adopted after leaving Missouri—were a renegade family of doubtful origin who had been petty thieves before the war, and who blossomed into full-time thieves and murderers under cover of the war.

Dave Allard, several times a murderer, had been tracked down and captured by Major Brionne. At his trial it had been Brionne's testimony that convicted him, and he was sentenced to be hanged.

Allard had lunged from his chair screaming, "They'll kill you, Brionne! My folks'll git you! They'll see you an' yourn burn! *Burn,* I tell you!"

Anne Brionne forced herself now to think calmly. There was no one else it could be, and she had always feared they might come someday, although James had derided Dave Allard's words as the wild threat of a man never sound mentally.

If these were the Allards, they would be looking for James. Without a doubt they expected to find him here, and they had probably watched Sam leave for the tavern, to be sure no one else was in the house.

Now they would try the other doors and the windows. When they tried the dining-room window they would find it open, for the night had been warm and she had left the window open, as she often did, for the breeze off the mountain. She had neglected to close it, and Malvernia would not have been in that part of the house after dinner.

"Mat," she said calmly, "I want you to go down into the cellar and leave by the old root-cellar door. Go to your cave and stay there until one of us comes for you. No matter what happens, no matter what you hear, stay there until either your father or I come to get you."

"Mother, I—"

"Do what you are told, Mat. That is the way your father would want it."

Still he hesitated. "Go," she repeated. "Go now."

A moment longer he hesitated—he did not like to see his mother standing there, so quiet and pale. Then he fled.

Anne Brionne's glance from the study window showed several horses under the trees ... she counted seven, and there might be others.

She unlocked the cabinet and took out the shotgun James used for hunting wild boar. It was loaded with heavy buckshot. Then she took out the pistol, a small derringer made in Philadelphia, that James had given her shortly after their marriage. It had two barrels, one under the other.

The doors from the dining room and the study faced the wide entrance hall on either side. She went up the six steps to the landing. From there the steps mounted in two wide, sweeping staircases to the second floor. On the landing there was a straight-backed chair.

Seating herself carefully, she arranged the folds of her robe about her, concealing the small gun in her lap under an edge of the gown. The shotgun she held across her knees. And there, her heart beating heavily, she waited.

This was her home. Here she had come as a bride, and Anne Brionne came of stubborn stock. Here she had lived in happiness. Here she had given birth to her son.

Generations of pioneer ancestors did not allow her to take the ownership of a home lightly. One had a home; one defended it. This was something she understood perfectly well.

She had never expected to be called upon to defend her home, although her grandmother had once defended a log cabin in this same state against an Indian attack. No, she had never expected it, but now that the moment had come she was prepared.

It was not an easy place to defend. She must frighten these intruders away, if possible. If poise and dignity could not do it, the shotgun must. In any case, Mat would be safe. The passage from the old root cellar, built for a pioneer house long ago, would allow Mat to escape to his river-bank cave. Even if they should find the passage, used only by Mat playing war games, they would not find the cave under the roots of the old oak.

After a moment, she rose. Taking a candle, she lighted it, and walked from place to place, lighting each candelabrum until the hall was as bright as for a party. Then she went back to the chair and seated herself as before.

There was no hope of keeping them out if they were determined to enter, but she hoped the shotgun might be sufficient to stop them and force them to leave. Yet deep within her she knew the man she had seen in the courtroom, shouting his threats, would not have been frightened off. Nor would his brothers or his cousins.

Fortunately, Malvernia was living in her own house behind the garden, and was not likely to be in danger. Her husband was off with the woodcutters, and she, too, was alone.

The footstep was faint, the door from the dining room opened ever so gently, and a man stood there. He was a big man with almost white hair, but he was young and strong. The muscles swelled the chest and sleeves of his shirt, a shirt that was soiled and worn, as was the vest he wore over it.

Slowly, he looked around, obviously amazed at everything he saw. A second man appeared, this one from the study door. He was slighter, and, if possible, he was dirtier than the first one. It was he who saw her.

He leaned forward, staring, as if unable to believe what his eyes told him. "It's a woman!" He spoke with astonishment. "Jest a-settin' there!"

Cotton Allard stepped further into the room. The newel post at the foot of the stairs bulked between them.

"You have come here to see Major Brionne," Anne Brionne said calmly. "He is not at home. This is not an hour at which we welcome guests. If you will come again, I am sure he will be most pleased to meet you."

"Now there's manners for ya." Cotton Allard was frankly admiring. "There sets a real lady. I allus wondered what them kind was like. Looks like we figure to find out."

"I would suggest"—Anne Brionne's voice chilled "—that you leave now."

Cotton Allard deliberately rolled his quid in his jaws and spat tobacco juice on the Persian rug. "I reckon with the Major gone we'll just have to make do with what's here." He turned toward the other man. "You tell the boys to take whatever they want from the house afore we set it afire. I aim to be busy right here."

"You tell 'em," the slighter man said. "I ain't a-goin' no place."

Cotton was cautious, keeping the newel post between himself and the woman. He had not yet seen the shotgun, which was partly hidden now beside her knee. Cotton could see only something dark by her hand, and something unnatural in her position.

The second man was less cautious. He stepped around in plain sight. Upstairs a door creaked faintly. So they had come up the back stairs too.

At that moment the slender, stoop-shouldered man rushed. Anne Brionne lifted the shotgun and shot him through the body.

In the hallway the boom of the gun was enormous. Anne saw the man caught in mid-stride, saw the expression of horror mask his face, and he slammed back as the charge hit him, and sprawled on his back on the floor.

Cotton Allard vaulted the banister, landing light as a cat on the landing beside her. From above, another man dropped off the balcony and the shotgun was torn from her. Coolly, she dropped her hand to the derringer, turned it on Cotton, and fired. It missed, and in almost the same instant Anne Brionne shot herself through the heart.

This it was that young Mat saw from the balcony where he had crouched, unable to leave his mother alone, but not knowing what to do. When Anne Brionne fell he gave a choking cry, and would have rushed to her.

Cotton saw him. "It's the kid!" he shouted. "Get him!"

Mat fled. Down the back stairs he went, down the steeper steps into the utter blackness of the cellar, but he needed no guide light to find the door to the old passage to the root cellar. He fled through the darkness, emerged under the trees, and glanced back toward the house just in time to see a man touch a candle to the curtains, those beautiful lace curtains his mother had imported from Alençon. The flames leaped high.

He crept down the bank, shivering and frightened. Behind the roots was his cave. He crept in and lay still, stiff and numb with shock.

The Allards ran from the house, clutching bottles of whiskey and brandy. Dimly, Mat heard their drunken shouts above the crackle of the flames. A long time later he fell asleep, remembering with horror the face of Cotton Allard, and of Tuleson, the one who had dropped from the balcony.

There under the roots Major James Brionne and Malvernia found Mat, curled up and asleep, on the following morning.

2

Major James Brionne glanced across the table at his son.

"Make the most of this, Mat. Soon you'll have to put up with my cooking."

"I like your cooking, pa."

The boy was subdued, too much so. In the four months that had gone by since the death of his mother, Mat had been very quiet. He talked only when spoken to, asked no questions, but stayed right at his father's heels as if he feared to lose him too.

Little by little he had told the story of that night —of his mother's quiet courage, of the awe-struck renegades; he had even told that last remark, heard as he hesitated briefly in the door, the remark made by Cotton Allard. "By the Lord Harry," Allard had said, "that there was a *woman!*"

But his words had come rarely, and Brionne had not tried to prod the boy into talking. There was no thought of returning to the estate the Major had loved so well. It was all too fresh in the boy's mind. What was needed was change, a complete and drastic change that would bring fresh interests, fresh demands.

"It is a lonely place to which we are going, Mat. We will see other people only when we go for supplies, but the town will be very small, I imagine."

James Brionne was a tall, wide-shouldered man of thirty-three, his face strongly boned, and darkened by sun and wind. He possessed that rare quality known as presence, and beneath it there was something else, for those who knew men of violence had a way of looking twice at James Brionne. Under the dignity, the poise, the military bearing there was something very tough and dangerous.

"We will be riding the steam cars, Mat. We will ride them for several days. You will be seeing a lot of new country."

"Will there be Indians?" Mat asked.

It was the first question, the first stir of interest he had shown.

"A few, I expect. I hope there will be no hostiles."

Suddenly a man in uniform was beside their table. "Major? The General is upstairs. He wishes to see you."

"We have come a long way, Colonel Devine, and the boy and I are tired." Brionne struggled to keep impatience from his tone. "I appreciate the General's kindness, but there is no more to be said."

Devine sat down abruptly. "He needs you, James. He is going to be re-elected, and he will need honest men about him. You know and I know that some of those around him are unmitigated scoundrels, but the General is not sophisticated in that sense. He needs somebody like you to weed them out."

"Somebody who isn't trusting at all. Is that what you mean?"

Devine took his cigar case from his pocket and passed it to Brionne, who accepted one. "You have a fine son, Major," Devine said. "Are you planning to let him go to waste in that confounded desert?"

"He won't be wasted, Colonel." Brionne spoke casually, but with a hint of iron in his tone. "He will learn a great deal out there, and he is a strong boy. It is a country for the strong, and it will make demands upon him."

"James, the General needs you," Devine reiterated. "You can write your own ticket. He would like you for his aide, but you can have a cabinet job ... whatever you want. He needs your judgment and your experience."

"Say what you mean, Devine. He wants a hatchet man. He wants somebody who will say no and mean it. He wants an axe that will cut, no matter where the chips fall."

Brionne stared down the room, thinking what this would have meant to him, and to Anne, only a few months ago. He knew very well what Grant thought of him, and he was one of the few men close to the President who had experience not only in the American West, but also abroad. He had conducted investigations that provided him with a unique background for the problems that lay ahead.

"The answer is no," he repeated. "I served in the Army and on detached service for twelve years. As a result I have lost my wife, my home, everything but my son. I did what needed to be done and I am not sorry, but now I am finished with all that. When I resigned my commission it was because I wish to be with my son ... and because I need time. Time to think, to read, and to watch my son grow up."

"Will you come to see Grant?" Devine asked. "After all, he is the President of the United States."

"Of course, I will come. I never served under a more complete soldier or a better general. I will come, but the answer will still be no."

Devine chewed on his cigar. Grant did need Brionne, but it was more than that. Devine was worried about Brionne himself. He knew something of the dark, bitter moods of the man, of the driving fury that was in him and that could be dangerous even to himself. This was no time for him to be separated from others, so soon after the death of his wife.

"I wish there was something I could say, James. Ethel is worried about you."

Brionne's mouth twisted wryly. "Colonel, that is one of the very reasons I am going away. I want to be free from pity, free from questions, free from sympathy and curiosity. I want to go somewhere where nobody knows and nobody cares. I have had too much of sympathy for now. Ethel is a lovely woman, but the first thing you know she will be trying to get me married off. You know how women are. She will be saying that I need a wife and that Mat needs a mother."

Devine smiled ruefully. Ethel *had* said that very thing not two hours ago.

They talked then of various things—of the coming presidential campaign, of conditions here in St. Louis, of the hotel where they were staying. Finally, Devine went back upstairs to Grant and the rest of the entourage.

Alone once more with his son, Brionne talked with him a little, and then he fell into a study. Was he doing the right thing? Was change the only answer? Was it an answer at all?

Night after night Mat had waked up screaming with fear. And he could not stand it to be left alone with only a woman to care for him, so fearful was he that the renegades might come back.

They had searched for him that dreadful night, and Mat recalled every footstep. There were times when they had come close enough for him to hear their sullen, muttering voices. He had seen them, he knew them, and he was the son of the man they hated.

The Southern Hotel's spacious dining room was one of the finest in the country, and the food was good. St. Louis was busy; it was the gateway to everything that lay to the west. There were people here who knew Brionne, and everyone knew who Devine was; they knew that if Devine spoke to him he must be important, for Devine was the President's closest friend and associate.

"Pa? Will I have a pony?" the boy asked.

"You will have a proper horse, Mat. A man's horse. We will be doing a lot of riding together, and where we are going there will be no roads, nothing but Indian trails, and very few of them."

At first, once his son had been found safe, Brionne had been seized by a sort of madness. There had been a pursuit, of course, and he had been among the leaders. The country had been shocked by the tragedy, and every man who could bestride a horse had been out with his rifle, hunting for the Allards, as they called themselves.

They had made a run for the mountains, but now they were without friends, even there. The hide-outs they once had used were closed to them, for this crime had been something even the hardest of the former guerillas could not stomach.

They had fought Brionne, but they knew him for a brave man, and respected him. They knew his wife too, and they would ride with no man who attacked women. The result was the Allards disappeared from their old haunts, and the story was that they had returned to Missouri.

Brionne refused to accept that. Harsh, relentless, bitter, he rode every trail, going alone into places where companies of cavalry had hesitated to go. Driven by the dark fury that Devine knew lay within him, he had ridden himself into exhaustion. Even his former enemies offered their help, but the Allards were gone. In the end he had realized his duty lay to his son.

"Do you know the place where we are going, pa?" Mat asked now.

"I've had a glimpse of it, son. It is a wild, strange, lonely land. Once you have put your eyes upon it, there is something in it that will never leave you. There are tremendous rocks everywhere—great, grotesque rocks ... and overhead the wide sky, the widest sky you ever saw, Mat. It is unbelievable."

He paused, thinking back. "I went into new country at your age, Mat. I was born in Canada, you know, and spoke nothing but French as a boy. When I was seven I went to Virginia to live with an aunt, and I grew up there, with occasional visits to Canada and to France.

"We did a lot of hunting and riding in the Blue Ridge Mountains when I was a boy, and I started school in Virginia. When I was old enough I entered the Virginia Military Institute, and later I spent a year at St. Cyr, in France."

It was an exciting story, and he told it the best he knew how, wanting to keep Mat's interest aroused. James Brionne had, because of his superior training and an uncle's influence, been commissioned a second lieutenant and sent to Indian country in the West.

Arriving just at the right moment, he went with Captain Stuart in pursuit of a party of Cheyennes who had attacked a mail party. Recovering twenty-four stolen horses and mules, they killed ten of the Cheyennes. Later, Brionne rode with Colonel Sumner against the Cheyennes and was in the battle of Solomon's Fork, and in the pursuit that followed.

In the next few years he rode on two dozen scouting trips into Indian country in Nebraska, Colorado, Wyoming, and Utah, but he was recalled and sent to Europe, without uniform, to engage in counterespionage against Confederate agents operating there, in France, England, and Germany.

The demand for officers brought him back to the States, where he took part in Grant's campaigns in the West, acquiring a reputation for his skill in moving and supplying large bodies of men. He was promoted to first lieutenant, then to captain, and finally to major. He had been among the first to see the possibilities of the railroads in handling troops and supplies; but near the end of the war he was once again sent to Europe when there were indications that one or more of the European nations might intervene on the side of the Confederacy. His command of French, as well as the friendships formed during his period at St. Cyr, served him well. When the war ended, he returned to his old home near Warrenton, Virginia, dividing his time between there and Washington.

"What will we do out west, pa?" Mat wanted to know.

"Oh, we'll prospect a little, catch a few wild horses, and we might even run a few cattle. We will cross that bridge when we get to it, Mat. Mostly we are going to see some new country, some wild country."

James Brionne pushed back his chair. "Now I must go to speak to the General, Mat."

"Pa, what state is St. Louis in?"

Brionne was considering the arguments he would offer to Grant, and spoke without thinking. "In Missouri, Mat. This is St. Louis, Missouri."

Mat stiffened abruptly, and Brionne looked down at his wide, startled eyes with sudden realization. "It is all right, Mat. There is not one chance in a thousand we will ever see the Allards again. And if we ever do, you must not be afraid. I will be with you."

He was thinking now that he dared not leave the

boy alone in his room, a prey to his imagination and to all the fears it could conjure up in a strange place. He would take Mat with him to see Grant. It might even help, for the General liked children.

He had started toward the stairway when he heard somebody say, "There goes Major Brionne. He is a friend of President Grant's."

A man seated in a chair near the foot of the steps looked up sharply at the words, his hard blue eyes staring right into those of Brionne.

Instantly, the man looked away as if fearful of being recognized. Brionne paused and the man got up quickly, folded his paper as he moved, and crossed the lobby toward the street.

Brionne hesitated. An old soldier friend? No. . . . He looked again, and saw that the man had paused in the doorway and was looking back at him. This time when their eyes met the man paused no longer, but went out and closed the door behind him.

Of course, people would be curious. Brionne had come to expect that, but in this man's eyes there had been such livid hatred mingled with what seemed to be fear that he was curious. But Colonel Devine was probably right. His training and his instinct had made him suspicious of everybody.

"Pa, come on!" Mat was saying.

That man's attitude disturbed Brionne, nagged at his consciousness. Yet the more he considered it, the more positive he became that he had never seen the man before.

He went up the stairs, and down the carpeted hall to the General's suite. Two stocky, powerful men stood guard outside. Both knew him from Washington. "Evenin', Major," one of them said. "The General's waitin' for you."

Grant sat behind a desk, the stub of a cigar in his teeth. His coat was unbuttoned, his tie somewhat askew.

He nodded shortly. "How are you, Brionne? Pull up a chair."

3

The train rumbled into the night. Outside, on the vast and empty plains, there was no light to be seen. Beside Brionne, on the seat next the window, Mat slept soundly.

The car was almost empty. Two seats ahead a young man lay on the seat with his legs in the aisle; his boots were down-at-heel, his spurs carrying the big rowels used by Mexicans or the Californios.

James Brionne had seen the man when he got on the train at some small station west of Omaha. He was a tall, loose-jointed young man with a shock of yellow-white hair and a look of dry amusement about him. He had winked at Mat, bobbed his head at Brionne, and promptly lighted a cigarette, which marked him as from the border country of Texas, where the habit had been picked up from the Mexicans.

The young man carried a beat-up Henry rifle; but with the practiced eye of the Army veteran, Brionne noticed the rifle was clean and well cared for. The belt gun was one of the heavy Walker Colts, a kind rarely seen.

There were half a dozen other persons in the car, including one young woman. Her clothes showed both style and quality, but they were a little worn. She was dark-eyed, and strikingly attractive in a well-poised sort of way. He wondered about her, and he tried to think of who she might be and why she might be going west.

Grant had been right, of course. He was running away, trying to escape not only the horror of his wife's death but everything that tied him to it. He was leaving Washington, his friends, the countryside he knew well. He was going toward . . . what?

And he could not say he was doing this only for Mat. He himself wanted to escape. He was going to a country he had seen only once, years ago, but it was a country that had never left his thoughts. He could still remember the stark loneliness of those towering pinnacles of rock, the brilliance of the stars, the expanse of the sky.

No land had ever touched him as had that wild and desolate desert, with its vastness and loneliness, the strange canyons, the stark ridges, the ruined ranges with their cascades of broken stone toppling into the valleys below. Deep within him something had always reached out with longing for that country.

He remembered an evening when he had led a patrol, scouting for a band of Indians that had stolen some horses. They came suddenly to the crest of a small saddle offering a fine view of the country beyond. He drew rein, astonished, and his men came up slowly around him, speechless with awe.

Before them lay a valley, a narrow corridor of green, deep in shadow now, a corridor between two rows of towering gargoyles, weird monsters shaped by wind, rain, and blown sand, carved from the native rock into these fantastic creatures of stone.

The trail had run out in the valley, and there was no reason to ride on, yet he felt drawn, impelled to go on into that darkening corridor. His men hung back, and his sergeant suggested tentatively: "Lieutenant, you can't tell me—no Injun would go down in there, not with night a-comin' on."

The man was right, of course. Reluctantly, Brionne had turned back. But this land spoke to him, whispering a song to his ears. When it was silent, and he sat unmoving, he heard the wind speaking to him from out of the distance, softly, plaintively. He knew then what was the song Ulysses heard when bound to the mast as he sailed past the siren islands.

The train came suddenly to a stop. There was a creaking of cars, a jolting, then silence, except for the distant sound of steam from the panting engine.

The tow-headed cowboy sat up, looking about. His eyes met Brionne's. "What's wrong?"

"I don't know." He glanced down at Mat. "I'll have a look."

The cowboy got up. "I'll go along."

Brionne hesitated, looking down at his son. The dark-eyed girl smiled. "Go along," she said. "I will watch over your son. If he wakes up I'll tell him where you've gone."

Brionne walked to the end of the car and stepped out on the platform.

Vast plains, rolling up into low hills, swept away on either hand. The single line of rails disappeared in the distance behind them. Holding to the handrail on the end of the car, he leaned out to look toward the engine. He could see the dark figures of two men who were talking, and the bobbing lantern of the conductor as he came back along the train, checking the cars.

Brionne swung down, the cowboy beside him. "What is it?" Brionne called softly.

"Fire," the conductor answered. "I smell fire. I figure one of the cars must've developed a hotbox or something. Maybe a cinder set the roof on fire."

The cowboy had been standing apart. "It ain't none of my affair, Mr. Conductor," he said mildly, "but if I was you I'd board up an' take this train a-sky-hootin' yonder. That there smell is grass a-burnin'. That's a prairie fire an' she's a-comin' thisaway!"

The conductor turned and stared at him in the darkness. "Sure enough," he said, "that *is* burnin' grass."

He turned and started a stumbling run back toward the engine, but even as he started the flames showed, a dull red glow against the sky.

"We can't make it," Brionne said. "We'd better backfire."

"Not here." The cowboy drew his gun. "There's a slough back up the line a ways. We'll need water." He fired into the air, and the conductor skidded to a stop.

"Back!" the cowboy yelled. "Back to the slough!"

There was an answering yell from the engineer, and the conductor leaped aboard the nearest car. Brionne swung up, catching the cowboy's hand as he jumped for the platform.

The engine wheels spun as they ground into reverse, and the train began to move. Already the horizon was dancing with a leaping line of flame. How far away was it? A mile—half a mile? In the darkness it was impossible to judge.

Grinding and roaring, the train backed up the line. Brionne went inside the swaying car. Mat was sitting up, his eyes wide and frightened. The girl was beside him.

"It's a grass fire, Mat," his father said. "You take care of this lady. She doesn't know about such things and she may be frightened. But stay inside the car."

He glanced around. "We'll need any help we can get." One of the passengers, a soldier in uniform, sat up, rubbing the sleep from his eyes. Brionne spoke to him. "Private, go forward along the cars and roust out all the men. Get buckets, anything that will hold water. These cars are made out of dried lumber and varnish. Soak them down!"

He threw off his coat and ran to the back of the car and jumped off as the train slowed. The slough was on the wrong side of the car to stop the fire, but there was a good water supply, and if need be it offered a shelter from the flames.

Brionne began running on the other side of the train, toward the fire. "Start one close in to the track," he said to the cowboy; "one that will get the nearest grass and that we can put out. I'll go farther out."

He could see the fire clearly now, great towering flames roaring over the prairie. When scarcely fifty yards out he stopped, knelt in the grass and tugged up a double handful. Lighting it, he waited until it was ablaze, then touched it to the grass. A flame leaped up, and he ran on, touching the grass until he could no longer hold his torch, then taking a second handful of grass. When he had a fire started the length of the train, he turned and started back, setting new fires inside the outer ones. The idea was to keep any fire from getting too large, but burning the grass toward the train to stop the big one that was coming.

Others were helping. A score of dark figures were alongside the track, throwing water over the cars. Others were burning grass, and putting out some when the flames got too high or too close.

It was desperate work. There is no work that will demand more of a man than fighting fire, for there is a desperation in it that is born of man's ancient fear and his present realization of the danger. Brionne had no sooner set the backfire than he was fighting to keep it under control.

The cowboy, who knew what to do and worked swiftly, had set a fire only six feet from the tracks, burning off a border that was easily controlled and soon burned out except for that edge that ate slowly back against the wind to meet the area burned off by Brionne's large fire.

But the great wall of flame came on; it was now only a few hundred yards off. The train stood between the burned-off portion and the slough. With the outer edge of the backfire burning slowly to meet the wall of flame, and with a margin of burned-off ground to protect them, all hands turned to drenching the wooden cars with water.

Several men got on top of the cars, and others passed buckets up to them. Still others were throwing water on the varnished walls of the cars. All were coughing from the smoke; leaves and grass blew over them, and blazing tumbleweed rolled close to them. The heat was intense.

Now the flames rolled up to the backfire and blazed furiously there, but they could go no farther. Around the ends of the backfire some flames tried to make their way around the island of slough and burned-off grass that surrounded the train, but these they could take care of more easily.

Within a few minutes it was obvious that the train was safe. Silently, the small group of tired men stood there for a moment.

Brionne found himself beside the cowboy. "Quite a fire," he commented dryly.

"Yeah. I've seen a few. This was a bad one."

The conductor came up to them. "I want to thank you men," he said. "Without you we'd have lost the train."

The cowboy chuckled. "I've come too far to lose my hair in a prairie fire," he said. "Pa allus said I was born to be hung."

He grinned at Brionne. "You move fast," he said. "My name's Mowry. Dutton Mowry."

Brionne shook his hand. "James Brionne," he said. "My son and I are heading west. Utah," he added, "or maybe over the line into Nevada."

"Headed that way m'self," Mowry said. "Where you leavin' the train?"

"Promontory," Brionne said. "We plan to locate somewhere south of there for a while and scout the country."

Mowry gave him a wry glance. "You don't look like no tenderfoot," he said, "but that there's a country to ride careful in."

They walked back to the train and slowly climbed aboard. The sudden emergency had changed the men from a trainload of strangers to a group of men who had joined hands in a common cause. Brionne glanced around at them, at their blackened, sweat-streaked faces. "It looks as if we should have saved some of that water for ourselves," he said, and a big Swede farmer grinned at him. The train started to move.

There was something about such emergencies that lasted, Brionne thought. No matter what happened to them afterwards, the men on this train would never be strangers to each other again. They had something in common and there was now a warmth between them, a knowledge of readiness to rise to an emergency, and each one of them felt better within himself for this victory they had won together.

Mat looked up at his father; his eyes were big. "I wanted to help," he said. "Miranda wouldn't let me."

"Thank you," Brionne said simply to the young woman. "I am James Brionne."

"I am Miranda Loften. You have a fine son, Mr. Brionne. I am afraid he comforted me more than I did him."

"You are going far?"

Her eyes became cool. "Not far, Mr. Brionne. Not far at all." Turning, she walked back to her seat.

"She's nice," Mat commented.

Brionne glanced out of the window. It was growing light. The last flecks of fire had died out, and now it was daylight.

The sun went behind heavy clouds, and there was a spattering of rain on the windows. The train's speed had slowed, for they were climbing a long grade. Brionne, suddenly restless, got up and strolled down the aisle, leaving Mat to watch the rain.

The big Swede grinned at him and two others spoke to him, commenting on the fire or on the weather. One man, a short, stocky man with a broad red face, looked up as he approached. "Heard you are getting off at Promontory. I keep a store there. If there's anything I can help you with, you just drop around."

"Thanks."

"Fellow back east was asking me about that golden spike they drove there at Promontory. Wanted to know if it was still there. I told him it would have been stolen long ago if they'd left it there. Why, there's men out there would steal the fillings out of your teeth if you left them around. And there's some would shoot you to get at them," he added.

Now the train slowed still more. Bending over, Brionne peered out of the rain-streaked windows.

The train was surrounded by a black sea of bobbing woolly black shapes.

"Buffalo!" he exclaimed.

The train stopped. The storekeeper leaned over to look out. "Hope it isn't like last time. We waited most a whole day while the buffalo passed ... millions, it seemed like."

Suddenly Brionne turned around. Two men stood at the end of the car, looking at him. One of them was a tall, round-shouldered man with wide hips made wider by the two guns he wore. His hat was battered, his shirt collar greasy with dirt, his drooping mustache tobacco-stained.

But it was the man beside him who drew Brionne's eyes, for he had a memory for faces. It was the man he had seen in the Southern Hotel in St. Louis.

Even as Brionne's eyes met theirs, the men turned and went through the door behind them.

The storekeeper followed his eyes. "They've got some horses back there ... ridin' in the baggage car. I don't know what else."

"I wonder where they were during the fire," Brionne commented. "I didn't see them."

"Come to think of it, neither did I."

The conductor paused beside them. "We'll be. in Cheyenne tonight," he said. "There's a live town for you."

"I hear there's some horses in the baggage car," Brionne said.

The conductor nodded. "Four men got on last night," he said. "They bought out the whole car. They've got six horses and a lot of gear. Wild horse hunters, they say."

Four men ...

Brionne went back to his seat. Mat had fallen asleep, and no one else was near. Opening his carpetbag, he took out his gunbelt and gun. He checked the load, and belted it on.

Then he sat back in the seat, facing toward the front of the train, and leaned back for a rest. He could watch the front of the train from where he sat.

Now the train had begun to move a little faster, for the buffalo were thinning out. Several times the whistle sounded, and each time the buffalo would trot a few steps, then subside to walking.

Mowry paused in the aisle. If he noted the addition of the gunbelt he offered no comment.

"Not many pilgrims aboard," he said. "If there was, they'd be shootin' the buffalo. I've seen twenty-five, maybe thirty men, shootin' all at once. Just killin'—not even able to get the tongues or liver. I never seen the like."

"They can run when they want to," Brionne said. "I've seen Indians hunt them on the run."

"Buckshot," Mowry said. "I favor buckshot. You can pick up a good shotgun ... a Wells-Fargo type express gun in Promontory. There's something mighty impressive about a shotgun."

Mowry drifted away, and Brionne sat back in his seat, the brim of his hat low over his eyes. ... Now what was that all about? Had they simply been talking about buffalo? Or was there something more?

4

As the train rumbled into the yards at Cheyenne, the conductor stopped by Brionne again. "We'll be in town an hour and a half," he said. "You and the boy best catch yourselves a bite. You'll find nothing else along the line that's worth the stoppin'. Not for a gent like you.

"The Cheyenne House ain't much," he went on. "Canvas partitions, and they sleep two in a bed. The food's worse than you'd expect. Hook's Pilgrim House is the best place to stay, but for grub the place to go is Kate Connor's. She's got an eating place close to the tracks, and you'll get the best. She cottons to youngsters."

The food at Kate Connor's was good, and the bustling, motherly Irish woman took Mat in hand as if she'd raised him from a baby. From time to time she studied Brionne. Finally, standing by the table, hands on her hips, she said, "Most folks I can spot right off, but you don't fit, mister. You don't look to be runnin' from nothing. You could be a gambler, but that ain't likely or you'd be stoppin' at one of the places down the street."

Brionne glanced at his watch. They had eaten well, and now it was nearing train time. He pushed back his chair and got up, and at that moment a bullet spattered glass and rang a deep gong from a Dutch oven hung on the wall near the door to the kitchen.

One quick hand pushed Mat to the floor, the other held a gun. Brionne, well inside the room, was crouching to look over the edge of a table and out of the window. He could see nothing in the darkness, but he waited for the flash of a gun ... it did not come.

Kate stared hard at him. "That was no drunken puncher, mister. That man figured on makin' you dead."

Brionne holstered his gun and stood up slowly. He smiled at her. "I don't believe so, Mrs. Connor. It was just a wild shot."

"You think what you like," she retorted, "but if I was in your boots I'd leave by the back door."

"Thanks," he said; "I believe we will."

Holding Mat's hand in his own left, Brionne eased out the back door and stood for a moment absolutely still, listening to the sounds of the Cheyenne night.

At least two music boxes were offering their jangling tunes to the night. Somewhere a door slammed and a squeaky pump started. A loud voice, with only the shadow of a tune, was singing a drunken song. Spurs jingled along the boardwalk in front of the restaurant.

Brionne squatted on his heels. "Mat, I don't believe that bullet was intended for us, but there are some rough men in this town. We will have to be very quiet ... like playing Indian. Do you understand?"

"Yes," the boy whispered.

"All right then. We are going down this alley and we are going to get back to the station and on the train. If they are wanting to shoot us, they will try to do it here, where nobody will be able to guess who did it. So we'll be very careful."

It would not be so bad, he reflected, if it were not for the boy. With no one to worry about but himself, he might have stalked whoever it was who had shot at him, and discovered what lay behind it. As it was, the sooner he got back to the comparative safety of the train, the better.

Skirting some barrels filled with garbage, Brionne found his way into the alley. There he hesitated, waiting to study the shadows. After a moment he started along, keeping to the deepest shadows, listening for the slightest sound. They made it to the back street.

Light from several open doors made rectangles in the darkness. His eyes had become accustomed to the darkness, and he studied the shadows. Crouching beside Mat, he whispered, "It's the doorways and the shadows we have to watch, Mat. Keep a lookout for movement. Many a time you will see nothing until something moves."

Diagonally across the street was another alley that led toward the tracks. From where he crouched Brionne could hear the heavy panting of the engine, and the occasional calls of the men working along the platform. It must be almost train time.

By now they knew he had left the restaurant by the rear door. If they were hunting him, they would be checking every route back to the station, and they were few. So far he had moved by the most direct way, and from this spot the most direct route was across the street into that alley . . . so they would not take it.

Quietly, his lips close to Mat's ear, he explained his reasoning. The boy was young, but the world does not always wait for the young to learn, and to Brionne's way of thinking no time was too soon.

Deliberately, he turned away from the street and worked his way with infinite care through the debris scattered back of the buildings. There were cans, bottles, old lumber, with here and there a fence to be crossed.

They came suddenly to the back door of a honky-tonk, and Brionne stepped up and opened the door. For an instant he stood there, studying the room.

Several card tables were busy, and there were half a dozen bartenders, although the evening was young. A red-skirted dance-hall girl with tawdry frills stood with her back to them.

And by the front window, with his back to them, was the man from the Southern Hotel. He was watching the street intently.

Brionne walked through the crowded room, still

holding Mat by the hand. Just as he came up behind the man at the window, the latter started to turn. Brionne's gun slid into his hand and the muzzle nudged the man in the back. The fellow looked around, his face sick with surprise when he saw who was behind him.

"Going back to the train?" Brionne's tone was polite. "This is a rough town. Maybe if we walked along together there would be less chance of trouble."

The man started to protest. "Now, see here!"

"Just start walking," Brionne said. "I have been shot at once tonight, and if anybody is going to try it again, we'll let them shoot at both of us."

Slowly, the man edged toward the door, then stepped out. "I am a dead shot, my friend," Brionne said, "so walk carefully. If you stumbled I might make a mistake and shoot you."

Scarcely a head turned as they left. Brionne's gun was held close, invisible to the eyes of those who glanced their way. Their slow parade down the center of the street and back to the train was not interrupted. At the train, Brionne said, "Turn around, my friend. I want to thank you for escorting my son and myself. There is no telling what might have happened without you along for company. I wonder who could be wanting to shoot me? Have you any ideas?"

"How should I know?"

The conductor came hurrying toward them, but hesitated when he saw Brionne. "Better get aboard, gentlemen. We are leaving in a few minutes."

"Is everyone aboard?" Brionne asked.

"Well . . . almost. There's been some delay, but I'm sure they'll all get here."

"Is it the gentlemen in the baggage car? Are they the ones who are late?"

"Well, now . . ."

"Let's just have a quick check. You first, conductor."

It took them a minute to walk through the two cars. No one was missing. Dutton Mowry, already slumped in his seat prepared for sleep, eyed them curiously as they walked down the car.

"No one missing," Brionne commented pleasantly, "so there's nothing to keep us, is there, conductor? Suppose you give them the high-ball?"

"Now, just a minute!" The conductor's protest was silenced when he saw the gun.

"Give them the signal, conductor, and if there are any complaints, I will stand responsible. I am Major James Brionne, and I think you will find your superiors will know me."

"Well, if you put it that way, I—"

"I *have* put it that way, conductor. We have delayed too long."

Reluctantly, the conductor stepped down and gave the signal. The whistle tooted and the cars jangled as the engine took up the slack. From the direction of town Brionne saw several dark figures sprinting toward the station. The conductor saw them, too.

"Too bad," Brionne said pleasantly. "They're going to be late."

The train started to move, rolled a bit faster, the whistle blew again. Under the train the rail ends began to clack and the cars creaked.

The men shouted, but the train continued to roll. Brionne lifted a hand and waved.

"Conductor, you may know this man." Brionne indicated his prisoner. "If you do, please persuade him that I wish to be left alone. I have no axes to grind, but I have no desire to be shot at. The next time shooting starts, if he is in the vicinity, I shall shoot him first."

"I don't want any trouble on my train," the conductor protested.

"And neither do I. My son and I are coming west because we love peace . . . and quiet.

"As for you, conductor, I imagine you will be very busy thinking up explanations to cover your rather peculiar association with those gentlemen back there, and to show why their horses are in the baggage car."

He indicated the door, and they entered the coach. The conductor and the other man walked forward; Brionne dropped into the seat beside Mat.

"Pa, were those men back there the ones who shot at you?"

"It's a reasonable assumption, Mat."

"But why?"

Brionne shrugged. "Mistaken identity perhaps. Or they might think I am doing some investigation for the government. There are people who know that I am close to Grant, and there have been some people who are stealing from the government, who may think that I am coming out to uncover their crimes. . . .

"Being shot at is distasteful," he added. "I hope we shall have no more of it, whatever the cause."

"What will those men do?" Mat asked.

"Catch the next train, I suppose. Now you'd better get some sleep. We have a long ride ahead."

Promontory was a row of weather-beaten shacks and tents facing the railroad. A sign proclaimed PACIFIC HOTEL: Soda Water. Next door was the Echo Bakery & Restaurant, Meals At All Hours. Further along were the Palace Saloon and the Sunny Side Hotel, which was a tent.

"We won't stay here," Brionne said.

Dutton Mowry came up and paused beside them. "You huntin' a horse? That there livery stable yonder usually has some good stock. I'm headin' thataway."

They walked along together. The street was dusty and crowded. Dozens of horses stood at the hitching rails in front of the saloons and hotels. There were many idlers, but there were few women.

The hostler looked up as they drew near. He threw a hard glance at Mowry. "You back again? Never did see a man who did so much runnin' around."

Mowry grinned at him. "Don't worry, Pat. I'm fixin' to light. I need a horse. So do these folks—and Pat, they're friends of mine."

Pat got up and led them back into the corral. Brionne walked out and the horses started to move. He watched them for a minute. "That all you've got?"

"Well," Pat said, "you can't ride more'n one at a time, can you? Yep, that's the lot."

"All right, I'll take the buckskin gelding with the black mane and the little dun."

Brionne had been watching the horses, and his

son as well. He had seen how Mat's eyes singled out the dun, and how the boy unconsciously moved toward the horse. The dun, far from being shy, pricked up its ears at the boy and stretched an inquisitive nose toward him.

Brionne also chose two sturdy-looking older horses for pack animals.

"What d'you want for the roan?" Mowry asked. "The big one?"

When they were back indoors and the deals were completed, Brionne looked across the desk at Pat. "And you forget you saw me, will you?" he said. "And anything else about me."

Pat gave him a surprised look. "You on the dodge? You sure don't look it."

"He ain't on the dodge," Mowry said, "you take it from me, but there's likely some folks comin' in on the train tomorrow who will be askin' questions."

"I don't know anything about you," Pat agreed. "I ain't seen nor heard of you."

They started back up the street, leaving the horses at the stable. At the nearest store Brionne bought a few items—some ammunition, bacon, flour, coffee, sugar, and canned goods, enough for several days. After packing it back to the livery stable he came back and at a second store bought another order of equal size.

He had stepped out on the street when he saw Miranda Loften. She was standing a few yards away, and two men stood in front of her. It was obvious that they had stopped her, and it was equally obvious that they had been drinking.

Brionne swung the two heavy sacks to the boardwalk. "Watch these, Mat. I will be right back."

He strolled up to where the girl was confronted by the two men. "Sorry to keep you waiting," he said gently, and taking her by the elbow, started away.

The men automatically stepped aside, and then one of them, more belligerent than the other, suddenly seized Brionne's arm. "Now, see here! What the—"

"Take your hand off my arm." Brionne spoke coolly, but the words were definite, and clearly spoken.

"Look, I was talkin' to that woman, an'—"

"The *lady* of whom you speak does not know you. In your present condition she does not wish to know you. I will tell you once more, my friend, take your hand off my arm."

Anger flared in the drunken man's eyes. "I'll be damned if—"

James Brionne, as those who knew him were aware, operated on an extremely short fuse. He brushed the arm away with his left hand, then crossed a solid right to the jaw. The punch was short, beautifully thrown, and it caught the correct angle of the man's jaw. He hit the ground, falling forward, as a man does when knocked out by such a blow.

Brionne looked across the fallen man, and said pleasantly, but with a cold look in his eyes, "Any comments? Would you like to make it two down?"

Suddenly sober, the other man shook his head. "Not me, mister. But when he wakes up you'd better be wearin' a gun."

"Tell him to forget it," Brionne replied. "If he had put a hand on this lady I'd have seen him hung . . . and you also. I would resent it if anyone disturbed this lady in any way, now or later. Do you understand?"

The man was flushing. "I'm sorry, ma'am. I reckon me an' Pete made a mistake." He gave Brionne a hard stare. "It ain't because of you, mister. We really did make a mistake."

Taking Miranda by the elbow, Brionne guided her down the street. "That man ... you didn't kill him?" she asked. "He hasn't moved."

"He'll have a headache, that's all." He changed the subject. "Miss Loften, what are your plans? Where are you going?"

"I'll be all right, thank you. I—I just don't know where to go tonight. I thought there'd be ... well, the hotels aren't like I expected."

He smiled. "They're for men, ma'am, and rough men at that. We must find something else for you. Let's go back and talk to Pat."

They crossed the street to avoid the group gathered around the man Brionne had hit, and went back to the livery stable.

"Sure'n my own Mary will have a place for you, miss," Pat said. "She'd not have you go elsewhere. She's a fine Irish lady, she is, and she will welcome you."

Brionne studied Miranda. "Miss Loften, permit me to ask, why did you come here in the first place? You do not seem the type of girl likely to come to Promontory."

"Oh, it's all right," she answered. "I have inherited a mine—a silver mine."

Pat glanced at Brionne. "A silver mine?" he questioned. "Near Promontory?"

"Well, actually it's south of here. It's a very rich

mine. My uncle told us all about it when he came east the last time, just before my mother died."

"I know of no silver mine around here," Pat said. "What might your uncle's name have been?"

"Brennan . . . they called him Rody, he told us."

Pat began to coil a rope, taking his time. Finally he spoke without looking up. "Miss, if you'd take an old man's advice, you'd get right on the first train east."

"But that would be foolish," she said. "Uncle Rody left me the mine. I don't know much about such things, but I do know something about business affairs, and I thought I'd look it over and decide whether to operate it or sell."

Brionne was watching Pat, and he was quite sure he knew what was coming. At least, he could guess what Pat was thinking. The West was full of mines; some of them were very rich, but most of them paid off in nothing but dreams and hard work. Everyone you talked to had a mine in mining country, and every one of them worth money . . . lots of money, or so they believed.

This girl had come west filled with hope, hope it would be cruel to destroy. "Mining is a man's business," he said quietly, "and the way business is done out here is not as it is in the East. Sometimes holding a claim is more difficult than finding one."

She smiled. "I expected you to say that, but Uncle Rody told me all about the mine—how many men he employed, and how many mules there were."

"Did he say where this mine was?" Pat asked.

She looked from one man to the other, suddenly distrustful—whether of their honesty or their belief was hard to guess. "I know where it is," she said. "He said it was near Salina."

Pat straightened up and put a hand to his back. "Miss," he said gently, "I doubt if there's more'n two houses in Salina ... never been there m'self. There's no mine workin' down thataway that's more than a one-man hole-in-the-ground. I surely hate to tell you this, but I knew Rody Brennan, and he never had any silver that I know of."

Her eyes were a little brighter. For an instant Brionne thought he saw her lip tremble. "Then where could he have gotten the money he gave us when he came east?" she asked reasonably. "When my father died he was in debt, and we had nothing. If it hadn't been for Uncle Rody, I don't know what we would have done."

"I remember when he went east," Pat agreed reluctantly, "but I never knew he took any silver with him. Fact is, I never knew Rody Brennan to have more than a mule and a saddle."

"Then you don't really know, do you?" Miranda Loften smoothed her dress. "I shall go to the mine and see for myself."

"There's been trouble down there, miss, Injun trouble. And even without Indians that's a rough country. Fact is, I think I heard that the folks who settled there at Salina had pulled out."

"Nevertheless, I shall go. Thank you, gentlemen. I am sure your advice was well intended." She looked now at Pat. "And now, if I may go to your house?"

He pointed. "Right through the door there, miss, and to your left. There's some roses at the door ... ain't doin' too well, but the wife likes them."

When she was gone, Pat said, "That fool girl will

get herself into all kinds of trouble. That's the wildest kind of country down there, and the Injuns have been cutting up something fierce. Anyway, Rody Brennan never had no mine that I know of."

"Where could he get that kind of money?"

Pat shrugged. "Now, there's a question," he said. "I don't know any way he could have done it honest. Rody drove spikes on the UP out of Omaha. By the time they were halfway across Nebraska he was a boss track-layer. When they drove the Golden Spike here at Promontory he was there with a bottle in his hand, and Rody was a fair-to-middlin' drinker when he set his mind to it.

"Rody drove stage to Salt Lake for a while, then he went off prospectin' into the hills, but he always came back to Promontory and Corinne. They've got a gun-shootin' marshal at Corinne. Daniel Ryan's his name, and he was an officer in the army durin' the late war. Rody was his friend.

"Come to think of it," Pat went on, "Ryan's the man the lady should talk to. He knew a sight more about Rody Brennan than the rest of us. But I never saw Rody with no money, not more'n he could be rid of in a day or two of drinking or gambling."

Brionne took out a cigar and lighted it. From where he stood, he could see Mat standing beside their supplies in front of the store. Actually, he had been there only a few minutes, and Brionne had been watching to be sure he was all right.

It was a busy street. Men crowded by, men of every stamp and kind: Scandinavian or German farmers looking for a place to locate, teamsters from the freight wagons, cowboys, railroad men, and drifters. A stage was loading to carry passengers south. The railroad had not yet put the stage out of business, although the tracks ran parallel to the road in places . . . but to the south there were no tracks as yet.

Brionne walked up the street to where Mat was waiting and picked up the heavy sacks. He placed the first one easily on his shoulder and took the other by the top. With Mat beside him, he walked back to the livery stable.

Pat spoke to them as they came up. "Come over to the house," he said. "You can eat with us."

Brionne hesitated, then agreed. Mat seemed pleased, for some reason. Did he fear his father's cooking that much? Or was it because he was tired?

"All right, Pat. We'll come." He paused. "By the way, what became of Dutton Mowry?"

"Him? He drifted off somewhere." Pat's manner was vague.

"Known him long?"

"A while. He comes and he goes, like all of these drifters."

Which told him exactly nothing, Brionne decided. Nor, judging by Pat's attitude, was he going to learn anything more from him.

Where had Mowry been when that shot was fired at him?

5

It was characteristic of James Brionne that he made his decision instantly, saying nothing of it to anyone.

Miranda Loften was there, with Pat's small family and two members of the train crew who boarded with them when in Promontory. One of the trainmen casually mentioned that they were going east with a lot of empties.

When supper was over, Brionne followed the trainman to the door to get a breath of air, and offered him a cigar.

"Those empty cars, you mentioned . . ."

"Yeah?"

"How much would it cost to carry my son, myself, and four horses to Corinne, or some point east of there? And say nothing to anyone?"

"If you're a friend of Pat's it will cost you nothing."

"One thing . . . I want to load up in the dark." He could see doubt in the man's eyes, and he explained. "Somebody took a shot at me in Cheyenne. I don't know why, but I think they've followed me here. I do not want trouble, with my boy along."

The details completed, they went inside again. Just inside the door Brionne said, "You must have known Rody Brennan—did he have any money?"

"Rody?" The brakeman chuckled. "Any time Rody had any money the bartenders got it . . . or his friends. That mick was the greatest guy you ever saw. He'd do anything for a friend. Why, he staked ol' Ed Shaw. Staked him time an' again. Every time Rody had a pay day Ed was there to get his part of it."

An hour later James Brionne and Mat were aboard the train for Corinne, and before daylight they left it just a few miles east of town. After two hours' sleep and a quick meal they headed south. It was a rough beginning for Mat, but Brionne wanted distance between himself and whoever had shot at him.

He had no theories beyond the obvious. It might be mistaken identity, or it might be somebody who remembered him from the war. There were a good many unreconstructed Confederates around. In any case, he was riding into country where he would not be likely to see them again, or to be seen by them.

For several days he and Mat rode and camped, loafing along the trails, stopping to fish in likely streams, moving as their thoughts willed. The days drifted easily into one another; the nights were cool, the air clear and sharp. Brionne hunted a little; he held to no fixed trail. Mat's cheeks turned from pink to tan, then to darker brown, with the sun and wind doing their work.

They saw no human beings, for they followed no traveled route. They did see antelope, deer, and beaver. Once they saw a bear. Twice, during the nights, mountain lions prowled. Each time Brionne frightened them away by moving about, but he kept the horses close in.

"We haven't seen any Indians," Mat said one evening as they sat by their campfire.

"They've seen us though, Mat. They've been watching us, and they're curious. Soon they will come down to talk, I think."

"Is this their land?"

"That's a good question, Mat. They were here first. At least, they were here before the white man came. But the Indian rarely claimed any fixed ground. Usually a wide area might be known as the hunting grounds of a certain tribe, but other tribes sometimes drove them away, and no boundary was recognized that could not be held by strength.

"They fought often among themselves over hunting grounds or areas where food plants grew. Sometimes they fought simply because they wanted to fight; often they fought for scalps. That's one of the troubles now. The older, wiser Indians have learned they cannot fight the white man, and they wish to live in peace; but the young braves need scalps to impress the Indian girls, so sometimes they go raiding and get the whole tribe into trouble."

The firelight flickered against the rocks, making dancing shadows. Brionne added a few sticks to the small blaze and listened into the darkness. They would be coming soon, if he knew Indians.

And suddenly they showed, just beyond the edge of the firelight. There were three of them. Brionne was sitting with his back against a rock, his rifle across his knees.

"There is food," he said quietly, almost as though speaking to Mat.

The Indians stayed very still, watching him. Then one of them came nearer, and the other two followed. "You ride far alone," one said. He was a tall Indian with a long face, scarred by an old wound.

"I am not alone. I have my rifle." He smiled then, and added, "I ride with my son. He is new to your land. I would see him become a great warrior, like yourself."

"He is young."

"But not too young to know the way of the wolf and the beaver."

Brionne answered their questions. They had been curious about him and his odd, wandering way toward the south. These were Utes, and members of their tribe had been raiding to the south, where he was going. Without seeming to make a point of it, he kept his rifle trained on one of them, shifting a knee from time to time.

They took food from the pot, and they drank coffee. They had eaten not long since, but an Indian would always eat again on the simple theory that it is best to eat when chance offers, for a man never knows when he will have food again.

"We go to stay in the land of standing rocks,"

Brionne said. "We will stay a moon, perhaps two. If we are among friends, it might be longer."

The Utes ate in silence for a time, then the long-faced warrior suddenly asked, "You are a pony soldier?"

"I was a chief among them, but there was no time for my son. He was growing up without me."

The Ute said something to the others, who looked at Brionne.

"You are right," Brionne said; "you did get away from me, but I was a young warrior then."

Surprised that he knew their language, they stared at him. He shrugged, "That was long ago. Now I come to your land as a friend."

"How do we know this?"

"Try me and see . . . as either friend or enemy."

"You have other enemies?" The scarred-faced warrior was prodding him, not with real animosity, but simply to see how he would react.

"Most of my enemies are dead, but there are some white men who are enemies to me."

The Ute chewed on a bone, then threw it aside. "I think you are friend," he said. "You speak well."

The Indian got to his feet, and Brionne stood up with him. Coolly, holding the rifle in his left hand, Brionne extended his right.

For an instant the Ute studied him; then he clasped his hand in a quick, sharp shake. The next moment they were gone like shadows, and Brionne moved quickly out of the firelight.

"Come, Mat," he said, "we will move camp."

"Tonight?"

"It is better." He threw a blanket over the buckskin. "Mat, I took a chance then, extending my hand to him. He thought of holding it while the others shot me. He thought of it, but he changed his mind."

"Why did he?"

"I don't know exactly, but you see I was holding his right hand, too, and I shoot very well with my left."

"You told them you wanted me to be a great warrior," Mat said.

Brionne looked at his son. "I want you to be whatever it takes to make you happy," he said; "and whatever you do, I want you to do it the best way you can, and then try to do it a little better still.

"I told him I was teaching you to be a warrior because it was something he would understand, and because it would immediately appeal to him. I do want you to be warrior enough to fight, if necessary, for what you believe, and for what is right."

As he spoke he was packing, staying well outside the circle of firelight as he did so. "We will move now, Mat. They might come back."

"You do not trust them?"

"Let's just say that I don't want them to be tempted," Brionne said.

Leaving the fire burning low, with a ring of earth banked about it to hold it in place, they walked their horses and went like ghosts from their camp. Two miles farther on, they made a dry camp, without a fire.

Brionne was restless. He was thinking of Anne tonight, as he had thought of her many times of late, wondering what she would have thought of his bringing Mat to this wild land. She had approved most of the things he did, and they had always been able to talk out the small points of disagreement. But he was sure he had done the right thing in coming to this country. Mat needed a new viewpoint, new surroundings, and so did he.

Then why was he uneasy?

The question came to him suddenly, sharply thrust into his conscious mind, demanding an answer. For he was uneasy . . . he was worried.

It was not the Indians. He had met them, and they were a possible danger. Others he might meet were a probable risk, too, but they were an understandable risk that one accepted when coming into this country. No . . . there was something else.

The mysterious shot in Cheyenne . . . Who could have fired it? And why?

Brionne was a coolly logical man up to a point, and he examined the facts now.

He was on no mission for the government. He was involved in no business deal. He had no axes to grind of any kind whatsoever.

He had no enemies he could think of, other than the Allards, who were somewhere back east. There might be some crack-brain who still wanted to fight the war, but that was unlikely.

Was it a case of mistaken identity? Possible, but doubtful.

He had assumed the shot had been fired by one of the men who rode in the baggage car, the men who were friends of the conductor, or at least were associated in some way with him. The man he found in the saloon was one of them, but he might not have been waiting for Brionne.

There was a chance that, knowing he had seen

Grant, these men feared he had been sent west to investigate ... what?

Grant was an honest man, but as Colonel Devine had implied, he was surrounded by many who were political high-binders, out for all they could get. Brionne was known as a trouble-shooter, and it might be they suspected he was going west to investigate some of the Indian agencies, or something of the kind.

But it was all too vague. In any event, he had left these things behind him.

There was a change upon the land now, a sense of something different. There was a new silence, a strangeness. Brionne welcomed it, and he watched his son with curious eyes. At last Mat said, "The air seems different. What is it?"

"Pines ... it's the smell of pines, Mat. But that is only part of it. It is the feeling of loneliness, the sense of quiet. We've moved away from people, Mat. This is the wilderness."

"I like it."

"So do I." He pointed toward the cliffs across the river. They ran east and west. "We will camp over there tonight, and find a way through them tomorrow. There are mountains beyond there, and we will find game."

He saw no tracks but those of deer. Occasionally they saw a buffalo. There were not many left in this country, and those few had drifted to the high meadows and the remote places.

Brionne made camp in a sheltered cove of the Book Cliffs. Gathering fuel for the fire, Mat stopped and spoke to him. "Pa, this looks like coal."

Brionne took the piece of rock from Mat's fingers. "It *is* coal," he said. "Is there much of it? Show me."

The vein was a wide one. He knocked off a few chunks with his propector's pick and carried them to the fire.

They had built it in a concealed hollow, and the rising smoke would have thinned out before it cleared the rocks around them. Brionne had killed a fool hen during the day, and they baked it in the coals. From time to time he walked out of the cove to listen to the night. All was still, with only the usual night sounds. Nonetheless, he continued to be uneasy.

At a back table in one of Corinne's nineteen saloons, Cotton Allard sat behind a bottle. His naturally red face was flushed a deeper red from a mixture of whiskey and anger.

"You had him an' you let him get away? He sure didn't up and fly through the air! Why wasn't you watchin'?"

"We watched. Only all of a sudden he wasn't there any more." It was the man from the Southern Hotel who spoke. "You ask Peabody."

Peabody Allard was the wide-hipped man who had been one of those who traveled with the horses.

"Hoffman's right. That Brionne is a sly one. I tell you he don't miss a trick. Him an' that boy of his'n, they—"

"That kid!" Cotton Allard exploded. "He knows the both of us, you know that? He knows me and he knows Tuley, and he ain't likely to forget it!"

"What I can't figure," Peabody Allard said, "is

how Brionne knew where to hunt for us. We didn't leave nobody behind—not nobody. There wasn't a way he could have known!"

Cotton stared at him angrily. "Then how you figure he got here? By accident? He knows ... I ain't sayin' how, but he knows!"

"We got to find him," Tuley said. "We got to kill him. We got to kill him an' the kid now anyway, else he'll find us."

"That reminds me," Hoffman said. "Rody Brennan's kin was aboard that train. I heard her say something about some silver mine or other."

"Rody's dead," Tuley said. "We got no call to worry about no kin of his. Leastways, not any girl kin."

"She was talkin' to Brionne," Peabody offered. "She sat with his kid when Brionne fought the fire."

Cotton mulled it over, hitching his gun around into his lap. He liked none of it. Brionne's showing up at Promontory couldn't be an accident. It was too pat, too easy.

"We got to keep nosin' around until we find where he's gone," he said finally. "You can bet somebody knows."

"Maybe he went huntin' Brennan's mine," Peabody suggested. "You say he was thick with the girl."

"I don't think Brennan had any mine. If he had, he'd of told us. You think he'd of stood all we did to him without tellin'? It don't stand to reason."

"I saw the silver," Hoffman said. "He surely had silver—some big chunks of it."

"He was no miner. You said so yourself."

"He might know somebody who was. How about

that old man he was forever staking to money? Ed Shaw—wasn't that his name?"

Cotton thought that over. "Well," he said at last, "the Gopher did say Shaw spent a lot of time down in the mountains east an' south of here."

He looked up, his flat, cruel eyes on Hoffman. "You round up that conductor friend. If Brionne left town on a train, he should find out. And Peeb, you go talk to that Irishman down to the stable where Brionne got his horses. He might know something."

Hoffman spoke up. "There was another gent on that train. Kind of a tow-headed man, looked like a Texican. Him and Brionne talked some."

"Forget him. If we paid mind to ever' gent Brionne talked to or ever' girl he made up to we'd never find him."

"I still think we ought to keep an eye on that girl. She didn't come way out here for nothing. I think she knows where that mine is."

"If there *is* any mine." Cotton's mean eyes were thoughtful. "All right. I'll have a look at her. But don't you forget, we got to kill that boy. If he grows up to have half the nerve his ma had ..." He paused, remembering. "That woman had sand. Chills me to think of her settin' there ... waitin'."

Outside, Hoffman started to walk up the street, then paused. "You be careful, Peeb," he said. "That sheriff they've got here is a tough one."

Peabody did not seem to hear. "That woman bothers his head," he told Hoffman. "Ol' Cotton's killed twenty-five, thirty men I know of—nine of them in face-up gun battles—an' he's killed four, five women, but none of them ever made him think twice. Only that Brionne woman."

"I heard Tuley speak of her. Cotton says he don't want none of her get growin' up to know who he is. I think he's more set on gettin' the kid than on Brionne."

"He'd better not be. I hear tell this here Brionne is hell on wheels with a gun."

They were silent for a few moments as they went up the street together. Then Peabody went on, "On'y there's nobody can use a gun like Cotton, not even ol' Tuley, an' he's mighty handy ... almighty handy!"

"You think we'll find Brionne?"

"Sure! This here's a big country, but no man can cut down through it without leavin' some notice of himself. If he's set on huntin' us down, we'll just give him the chance."

"There's one thing," Hoffman commented after a moment. "Brionne don't know Cotton ... nor Tuley. He never laid eyes on them."

"On'y that kid."

"I don't like that," Hoffman muttered. "I never killed a kid."

"Nits make lice," Peabody replied shortly. "What difference does it make?"

They separated at the corner. Hoffman hesitated, thinking, then he started for the Golden Spike. That was where his friend the conductor hung out. If Brionne had used the railroad he would have heard some talk of it.

A tow-headed cowboy, the one who had helped fight fire when it endangered the train, was loafing on the corner. Another drifter. The town was full of them.

6

Alone in her room at Pat Brady's place, Miranda
Loften counted over her money.

Seventy-four dollars and fifty cents . . . That, and
nothing more.

That was all that stood between herself and whatever happened to a girl who was without money, in a
place where there were no jobs for women.

Of course, there was her father's gold watch and
her mother's ruby and diamond ring.

It was costing her just fifty cents a day to live at
the Bradys' and Pat would let her have horses at a
dollar a head per day. When she started out she

PRESENTING

The Louis L'Amour Collection

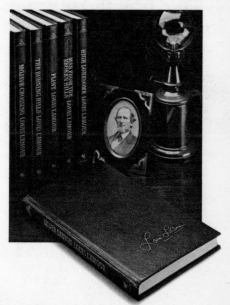

Explore <u>Silver Canyon</u>,
your first handsome hardcover
Collector's Edition
for 10 days <u>FREE</u>

Enjoy the best of Louis L'Amour in special volumes made to last as long as your pleasure

As a reader of Louis L'Amour's tough and gritty tales of the Old West, you'll be delighted by The Louis L'Amour Collection— a series of hardcover editions of Louis L'Amour's exciting Western adventures.

The feel of rich leathers. Like a good saddle, these volumes are made to last—to be read, re-read and passed along to family and friends for years to come. Bound in rugged sierra-brown simulated leather with gold lettering, The Louis L'Amour Collection will be a handsome addition to your home library.

Silver Canyon opens the series. It's the memorable tale of Matt Brennan, gunfighter, and his lone battle against duelling ranchers in one of the bloodiest range wars the West had ever seen. After *Silver Canyon* you'll set out on a new adventure every month, as succeeding volumes in the Collection are conveniently mailed to your home.

Receive the full-color Louis L'Amour Western Calendar FREE—just for looking at *Silver Canyon*. Like every volume in The Louis L'Amour Collection, *Silver Canyon* is yours to examine without risk or obligation. If you're not satisfied, return it within 10 days and owe nothing. The calendar is yours to keep.

Send no money now. Simply complete the coupon opposite to enter your subscription to The Louis L'Amour Collection and receive your free calendar.

would need food, blankets, and some kind of a weapon.

The trouble was she had no idea how long it would take to get to the mine, or just how far she would have to travel, and she was afraid to ask anyone. If only she had dared trust that man ... the tall man with the little boy. He seemed so sure of himself, so positive about where he was going and what he was going to do.

As for Mat ..., despite herself, she worried about him. He was such a little boy to be going into that wild country. Did his father realize how young he was to face such hardships and dangers?

Nobody seemed to believe in Rody Brennan's silver mine. He was a man everybody had liked, a man who talked and spent freely. And nobody seemed to have any secrets in this country. There were too few people for any of them not to be known to the others. Nobody believed in Rody Brennan's mine, but Miranda Loften had never known Uncle Rody to lie.

He had told her where the mine was, even how to get there. He had left them what money he had and gone back west on his railroad pass. He might, she admitted to herself now, he might have exaggerated the importance of the mine and the number of men working there. It would be like him to do that to convince them it was no hardship for him to give them the money.

But it was odd that no one out here even knew of the mine, or knew that he had any interest in one. Come to think of it, the thing he had been most explicit about back home was its location. She had made no further inquiries here, but whenever she could she steered the conversation to mining, but there was never a comment on Uncle Rody when the talk involved mining.

She might, she was thinking, be able to sell the ring. It might give her money enough to hire horses, and to get the supplies she would need. Yet deep inside her was a kind of fear at the thought of relinquishing the ring.

Her lips trembled, and she sat down stiffly on the edge of the bed. ... Suppose there was no mine? Suppose Uncle Rody had just gotten that money some other way—somewhere, somehow—and had told them there was a mine so they would accept the money?

Yet, if that was the case, why the careful directions?

Moreover, there was her fear about the ring. It was a family heirloom, and her mother had told her it was valuable; but Miranda doubted that her mother knew that much about jewelry. That was really what she was afraid of—suppose the ring was not really valuable—suppose it was worth nothing.

She had to find the mine, and to find it she had to risk everything she had. If she could not find it within a few weeks she would have to give up, and she would not have even the money for a ticket back.

She could not bring herself to say a ticket *home*. It was no longer home. It was only one of several cities in which she had lived as a child, and it was the place where her mother was buried. There was nothing there for her, nobody ... only a few people who had known her to speak to, a few casual friends of her mother. Nobody who had any interest in her, nobody in whom she had any interest.

She was alone.

The shadows grew long, but she did not light the lamp. She still sat stiffly on the edge of the bed, frightened at what was before her.

Yes, to find the mine was her only chance. Without it, there was nothing. There were no jobs for women in Corinne except in the dance halls and in the cribs behind them. There were few other jobs available anywhere except as household help, which she could do, but which she shrank from except as a last necessity. Even that would mean she would have to go somewhere else, to a city where people hired household workers.

She would talk to Pat tonight. She would arrange for horses, and she would ask his advice on what she would need to take with her.

She got up and left the room. Tonight only Pat and Nora Brady were in the house, and they had been talking about her. She knew that as soon as she joined them.

"Pat"—he had insisted she call him that—"I shall need a horse to ride, and a pack horse. I am going out after that mine."

"Ma'am," Pat said gently, "you better realize what I'm sayin'. There just ain't no mine. Nora an' me, we knew your Uncle Rody. We been going back over the years after he came west ... ma'am, he didn't have time to find any mine! We just been sittin' here figurin' it out. He was never out in those hills, never in his life! At least, not far enough or long enough.

"I can tell you how long he worked for the railroad, when he hired out to drive stage. . . . Ma'am, except for that trip back east, Rody Brennan was always right where folks could see him."

So there it was. She felt the fear growing inside her. She had always, down underneath, been afraid it was too good to be true, just as she was afraid the ring was worthless.

But she lifted her chin a little now and said quietly, "Pat, I believe Uncle Rody. He told big stories sometimes, but he never lied to me."

She took up her cup of coffee. Holding it carefully with both hands, she went on speaking. "I do not have much money, Pat, but I have a ring. If you would buy it from me . . . or better still, let me have the horses and hold the ring for security . . ."

"Miss, didn't you hear a word I said? There's no silver, there's no mine. There couldn't have been."

"Uncle Rody Brennan never lied . . . not to me. He said there was a mine, and I believe him." She looked earnestly at them. "There just *has* to be a mine. It is all I have."

"Now, look here," Pat began.

Nora stopped him. "Be still now, Pat. Let a woman talk. It's like this. Pat an' me, we've taken to you, Miranda. We've no daughter of our own, so s'posin' you stay on with us, just like you have been."

"Why, there's no tellin' who might come along! There's many a handsome laddie comes by this way, and the best of the lot come to eat with us. You could have the pick of them, an' hereabouts there's mighty few girls, and none as pretty as you."

"Thank you, Nora—it is good of you. But no—I have to find that mine. I have to. I want to marry, but on my own terms, not just because I have to have someone to take care of me."

Pat sat back in his chair and stuffed his pipe. Loaded it, might have been a better term, for the fumes from that pipe had been known to send grizzlies back into the deepest canyons, to stampede buffalo, and even skunks were repelled by it.

"Miss, have you got any idea what you're takin' on?" he asked after a moment's silence. "There's thousands of square miles out yonder, filled with all manner of varmints, four-legged or two.

"When the railroad ended at Promontory it spilled all the workers and the camp followers and the trash that lived at the hell-on-wheels towns at the end of the track, it spilled them all loose on the country.

"Those with money rode the cars out, east or west, but a mighty big lot of them were caught with little or nothing, and they stayed on to rob, to kill, to get along any way they can. And those woods are full of them."

"I am going," Miranda said firmly.

"There's Utes, too. Indians, they are, and pizen mean."

"You can't talk me out of it, Pat," she said quietly.

"Then we'll just have to find somebody to ride along. It's a pity you couldn't have gone with Major Brionne."

"*Major* Brionne? Major James Brionne? Was that who that was?"

"You know him? I saw the name on some of his gear."

"I know the story." Suddenly she was thoughtful. That poor little boy! Slowly, remembering it as she had read it in the papers, she told the story of the attack on the Brionne home, the death of his wife, and of the search for the Allards. "He is a very famous man," she said.

"Aye," Pat said thoughtfully, "I remember it now, although it's been few newspapers we've seen out here."

No wonder that little boy had been so quiet at first! She remembered how he had snuggled against her when the flames were coming close. At that moment little Mat must have been remembering the flames when his home burned. Shuddering, she put the thought from her mind. She would not see them again ... somehow the thought gave her a sense of loss, of loneliness. And that was foolish. She had spoken only a few words to James Brionne.

She took the ring from her purse, and handed it across the table to Pat. "Will you buy that? Or accept it for security?"

He shrugged. "Miss, I don't know nothing about such things. If this here is worth what it looks like, there ain't money enough in town to buy it; and if it ain't—well, it just ain't worth much of anything."

"Will you take it for security?"

Pat looked up at her, smiling. "Miss, you been livin' in the East too long. Out here we do business on character, not on notes or security or the like. I like you and I think you're a solid person, so I'll stake you to the horses an' gear you need. You pay me when you can."

He passed the ring back to her. "You keep that."

She shook her head. "No, Pat. Something might happen to me. You keep it for me. I shall want to leave the day after tomorrow."

"I got to find somebody for you," Pat protested. "That may take time."

"There's a man who was on the train," she suggested. "I have seen him around and he doesn't seem to be doing anything. He worked with Major Brionne to put out that fire, and he seemed very competent. I wonder if—"

Pat's face was expressionless. "I know the man you mean. I'll talk to him."

Outside, he paused in the darkness and lit his pipe. Odd that she should pick on Dut Mowry . . . of all people.

Pat Brady walked through the darkness toward the stable. He always made this late check to be sure everything was all right. His night hostler was a good man, but old, and Pat liked to keep an eye on the comings and goings in town.

He had almost reached the stable when he heard voices, and he slowed down, never liking to come up on anybody in the dark.

There were three of them, and they were speaking in low tones, but Pat could hear what they were saying.

"He talked the trainman into carryin' him on past Corinne. They dropped him there, and him an' the kid took off south."

"Salt Lake?"

"I reckon not. He was packed for travel. I figure he was headed into the Uintahs."

"That's our country. All right, boys, we've got him. We'll light out, come daybreak."

They walked out of the alley into the street, and for a moment Pat saw them clearly. All three were strangers, but he had seen at least one of them before. He was a big man with a wide, deep chest and yellow-white hair. He had a flat, dangerous-looking face, and Pat Brady had seen him around several times. He was the man they called Cotton.

At the stable all was quiet. The hostler said no newcomers had come into town, nobody had left. Dutton Mowry? He hadn't seen him.

Pat drifted down the street, looking into several saloons. At last, almost at the end of the street, he saw the faint glow of a cigarette, and walked toward it. His guess was right.

Mowry was leaning against the awning post, and he spoke around his cigarette. "Howdy, Pat. Late for you, ain't it?"

Briefly, Pat Brady outlined Miranda Loften's proposal. Mowry listened, offering no comment. Finally he said, "You say Rody Brennan never had any silver?"

"Not that I know of. How could he? He was around all the time. I mean, he was a man who talked a lot, and he'd have talked about that. Anyway, he was busy every day. He never went off to do any prospecting."

"Drivin' stage like that he must've knowed a lot of folks."

"I suppose he did."

"Nice feller, they say. I've heard talk about Rody Brennan. Folks said he was a free-handed man."

"Give you the shirt off his back," Pat said. "Never asked nothing of nobody, but if you were in trouble, Rody was the man to go to."

"An' this girl says he never lied to her?"

"That's what she said. . . . Will you help her?"

Mowry tossed his cigarette into the dust. He stood

for a moment watching the dying glow. "No," he said finally.

"Well," Pat said, "I tried." He turned to go, then paused. "Brionne, now. Was he a friend of yours?"

"A good man. . . . Why?"

Brady repeated the conversation he had heard. Mowry listened, lighting another smoke. "Called him Cotton, you say? A big feller?"

"That's right."

Mowry smoked in silence. "You don't need to worry none. I figure that Brionne feller is a pretty handy man. I mean, if a body was figuring on picking a fight, he'd better not choose him. I think not."

Pat Brady turned away. "Good night, Dut. I'm off to bed."

"Pat?"

Brady stopped.

"You tell that lady I'll go with her. You tell her that if Rody Brennan had a mine, we'll find it."

Pat Brady walked away down the street, and Dutton Mowry finished his cigarette. Maybe he was being a damn fool. Maybe he was just getting himself into a lot of grief, playing shepherd to a tenderfoot girl in wild country, but he had a hunch, and he was a man who played his hunches. Besides, when you came right down to it she seemed level-headed. There was something substantial about that girl, something that made you think she was one to ride the river . . . and they didn't come too often.

"Dut," he said to himself, "you've opened your big mouth and bought yourself a packet of trouble."

Still, he did not feel depressed. He was pleased with the decision he had made, although he was not quite sure why. He was playing a wild-haired hunch that just might pay off, and it was based on two little threads of information that had come to him in the past few days. Two threads that might not tie in at all, but if they did—and his hunch was that they would—he would be there when all Hell broke loose.

"Dut," he repeated, "you've bought trouble, but when didn't you have trouble? And when did you fight shy of it?"

One thing remained. Major James Brionne had better watch his back.

7

The stream chuckled over the stones, sunlight glancing from the water. Downstream a few feet the water rippled quietly about a dead branch that hung suspended in the clear water.

Mat Brionne sat on the bank under a dappling of shadow from the leaves overhead. He was fishing, but not very seriously. He was just sitting, eyes half closed, suspended in time, and he was happy. He was deeply, richly content.

There was the sound of the water and the sound of the wind in the trees, a far-off sound like that of a distant train rushing over the rails. Across the stream, only a few feet away, two squirrels were playing among the leaves, making soft, scurrying sounds.

Not more than thirty yards away through the trees, Mat could hear his father as he worked around the camp. And sometimes he could hear him singing as he worked.

It was three weeks since they had left Promontory, and they were in the foothills of the Uintahs. Brionne had planned to go further south, but had changed his mind suddenly and headed deeper into the mountains. Mat studied about that.

His father had long wished to come back to a certain area of Utah, so why had he suddenly changed his mind? Not that Mat minded one little bit. He had never seen country more beautiful than this, and he liked loafing along day after day. But it seemed to him that his father was acting strangely.

The way they moved, for example. Just when they had found a good camp, they would move, all of a sudden, and without warning. And each move took them deeper into the wilderness. Mat speculated about it, for usually the moves came after one of his pa's night-wandering spells.

James Brionne would make camp, fix supper, talk a bit, and then get Mat settled in his bed. After that he would say, "I'll be back in a few minutes," and he would walk off into the night.

He was never gone long. He would suddenly reappear, look around to see that all was well—Mat usually pretended to be asleep—and then he would go off again. And each time he went armed.

Sometimes he would go out in the first light of dawn, and at those times he would find some place with a view, and study the country around.

It had started about a week after leaving Promontory, when they made camp one night with three prospectors. They had come drifting in out of the night, calling out to the camp fire.

"That's the proper way," Brionne explained to Mat. "Never approach a man's campfire without announcing yourself. You might get shot."

Mat liked the three men at once. One of them was a youngish fellow with sandy hair, freckles, and a big Adam's apple, and he was full of jokes and easy humor. The others were older, and they too were filled with stories, and they were quick to work around camp.

Brionne listened. He had advised Mat about that. "If you listen, you learn. If you learn to really see things and to really listen, half your troubles are over."

These men were talking about the country. Mat, who was listening well, and trying hard to pick out the important details instead of just hearing the stories, soon discovered that his father was leading them on by his questions. Brionne was learning about the country, the people he might expect to find, the stories of other people who had wandered there, the Indians, and everything.

The three men were Paddy O'Leary, Tom Hicks, who was the redhead, and Granville. Granville was the quietest of the three, a tall, slender man who moved easily, and relaxed whenever he sat down.

O'Leary was the talker. "Shaw was the man," he said; "nobody knew this country like him. Used to like to camp down in Nine Mile. Said he could read all those inscriptions and pictures on the wall."

"I figure he lied," Hicks commented. "That's just

Injun writing ... like a feller does with a pencil when he's got time on his hands."

"Shaw wouldn't agree with you," O'Leary insisted. "He spent a lot of time figuring about those pictures. He said one day they'd make his fortune. He had it figured that whilst lots of them were just written for the gods, or for hunting charms or the like, some of them had a story to tell. He used to show us a silver armband he'd found.

"He'd say, 'Now where do you suppose that there silver came from?' And he'd tell us how he'd found some small fragments of broken rock in some of the caves or Injun houses along Nine Mile. He'd say that rock didn't belong there, and he had it figured it was rock that had come from the same ground the silver did, that the Injuns worked the silver out of it. He used to bet he'd someday find that silver mine."

Granville was the thoughtful man, and one evening after the subject of Shaw had come up again, he commented, "I think Ed Shaw was right. And I think he found something."

Brionne glanced over at him. "Really?"

Granville smiled, his eyes glinting with a kind of amusement as he looked back at Brionne. "Really," he repeated, and then he added, "One day he just up and took off. Shaw was a lucky one. He had somebody grub-staking him, and I think he went down to Corinne, got some more supplies, and followed his hunch."

"It didn't get him anywhere, either," Hicks said dryly. "He's dead." And then suddenly he spoke again. "Say, maybe we could trail him to where he went! He'd have a claim staked, but he's not alive now."

James Brionne took a cigar from his pocket. "Whatever Shaw had would go to his family, if he had any, and to whoever grubstaked him."

"If they could find the silver," O'Leary agreed. "An' that ain't likely."

Mat Brionne remembered that night well, because it was since then that their manner of travel had been so strange. Not only had they several times moved suddenly, often after dark, but several times they had changed direction.

"Always watch your back trail, Mat," Brionne told him. "Country looks a whole lot different when you are facing the other way. Landmarks that show up very well when you're going east may not look at all the same when you're going west."

Mat remembered that, but he thought that his father took a lot of time studying his trail, and it was always from some vantage point where he could see a good bit of it. Mat often looked back with him, but he could never see anything special.

The fact was that James Brionne was quite sure that he was being followed. Mat had guessed right when he decided his father must be looking at something besides landmarks during those long periods of studying his back trail.

His sudden changes of direction had been for two reasons. First, to see if he was followed, and then, if so, to try to throw them off the trail. By now he was sure of the first, and he felt that he had not slowed them down even by a little. So they were fair country trackers, then. That posed a different sort of problem.

So tonight he got up before daylight and packed swiftly, and when Mat woke up everything was packed except for his bed. The coffeepot was still on the fire. Until this trip Mat had never been allowed to drink coffee, but there was no milk to be had out here. There was a piece of broiling meat on a stick over the dying coals. He ate that and drank coffee, and then his father watched him mount up.

They turned away from the camp, rode out on a rocky ledge, and switched around and rode right back along the ledge and into the water. Riding upstream for half a mile, they came out on another such ledge and rode through a thick stand of trees, where the floor of the forest was covered with leaves and where even at midday it was shadowed, as if it were twilight.

All day they switched back and forth. Once they stopped for a few minutes to let the horses catch their wind after a steep slope, and Brionne broke out some pemmican and gave a good-sized chunk to Mat to chew on as he rode. Not until late afternoon did he pause to let the horses graze.

There was no chance of watching the back trail now. Most of the travel was in forest, and even the character of the trees was changing. Now, as they climbed higher, the trees were mostly evergreen. Here, too, they ate pemmican. They drank cold water, then mounted up and rode on again.

Although their change of direction was often due to the character of the ground, they continued to ride uphill. It was long after dark before they made a cold camp behind a clump of aspen. Mat was very tired, and he was almost falling off his horse when Brionne reached for him.

Brionne prepared Mat's bed, pulled off his boots and pants, and tucked him in. During all this time his eyes rarely left the horses, but they grazed contentedly, seemingly glad to stop. Not once did they look up or prick their ears.

Brionne always enjoyed a problem, and he had one now. Ed Shaw had been prowling around the back country for a good many years, and he had spent some time trying to interpret the picture writing, or whatever it was, in Nine Mile Canyon. Suppose there had been a map to the silver mine that had been used by the Indians?

Maps are of many kinds, and few primitive maps looked like those to which Europeans or Americans were accustomed. In the South Pacific they were sticks with shells tied on them to represent islands, the sticks indicating prevailing winds or ocean currents; but many ancient maps were done in pictures. There was a symbol for running water, there were symbols for peaks . . . suppose there was a symbol for silver?

The old man had known this country, and he might have found something. Somebody had been supplying him with cash, and that somebody had apparently been Rody Brennan. Therefore Brennan need not have gone into the mountains at all. Ed Shaw would have worked on Brennan's grubstake; and he must have brought out some silver that he turned into cash. With Shaw dead, Rody Brennan became the legitimate owner of the mine—if there was one.

Little by little, James Brionne isolated the few facts he had obtained from the various conversations he had heard. Out of them had come Shaw's apparent angle of approach to the mountains, and some hint of the time he had taken. Vague as these things were, it was interesting to speculate on the direction he might have followed, and the possible location of the mine.

After adding a little fuel to the fire, concealed in a small hollow and shielded by the aspen, Brionne took up his rifle and went to a rock that jutted from the side of the mountain. Earlier he had noticed that it would be simple enough to climb up there, and once there, he sat down to survey the country around.

Looking down, he could see the campfire and the small figure of his son. Looking outward, he could see only endless blackness of forest, the blue-black of the star-studded sky, and the great bulk of the mountain, rising behind him and on his left.

For a long time he studied the night—not the stars, but the forest blackness. When he caught the gleam, it was out of the corner of his right eye, miles away and much lower down.

Watching, he saw it again . . . and again. A campfire. His point of vantage could scarcely have been better. The air was clear, and he was high up. The fire might be ten miles away, but it was probably less.

Brionne considered the country between, trying to recall how much of a trail he had left behind. He was rising to leave the rock when he glimpsed another light, not quite so far off, and a little higher up the mountain.

He studied that light through his glasses, but they helped him not at all. The distance was too great, and they merely showed a somewhat larger light, unidentifiable even as a fire. Now who could that be?

Returning to camp, he arranged his blankets and

lay down, clasping his hands behind his head. For a long time he considered his next move, then at last he fell asleep, remembering Anne, as he had seen her last . . . too long ago.

The second light Brionne had seen was the campfire of Dutton Mowry and Miranda Loften.

Knowing the way to go, they had moved faster than Brionne. They were not following anyone, and were not expecting anyone to be following them. Mowry was a good man on a trail, and he had chosen good stock for them. They were higher up the mountain than the Allards, and about three miles ahead of them.

The trail they had followed was an old game trail, used occasionally by Indians. Two days ago, their trail had been the same as that of the Allards, and Mowry had noticed the fresh sign, and had taken time to learn the track of each horse. Within a few minutes after coming upon the trail he knew one of the men was Cotton Allard.

Then the trail, as designated by Miranda, took them farther up the slope. He turned to her now and indicated the rifle she carried.

"Can you use that?" he asked.

"Yes."

"Don't ever go anywhere without it. Not in this country. And if I say jump, you jump—don't ask why. If you take time to ask, it may be too late."

"All right."

"How much farther is this mine of yours?"

"It's up on top . . . among the lakes. Another three days, I think, if nothing stops us."

He considered putting the fire out, but instead he

banked it; then he left it and went to his blankets. "Get some sleep," he said to Miranda. "We've got a rough day ahead. We're going to try to cut three days to two, if we can."

At her questioning glance he added, "We ain't the only ones up here. Brionne is up ahead of us."

Startled, she stared at him. "Looking for silver? He *can't* be!"

Mowry shrugged. He looked at her, his eyes amused. "Why not?"

"I—I just don't believe it."

He chuckled. "I was only funnin'. That is, if he is huntin' the silver, you must've told him more than you thought."

She racked her brain. "No ... no, I told him nothing. Nothing at all."

"He ain't the on'y one." Mowry settled into his blankets. "The Allards that are huntin' him, they're out here, too."

She sat up. "Are you sure?"

"Uh-huh ... and so's he. If the Allards are smart as they're supposed to be they won't foller him any further. They might catch up with him."

8

With the first gray light of morning, Brionne squatted beside the small fire, drinking coffee and studying the steepening slope before them.

There was no trail up it. Here and there were rocky outcroppings; there were clumps of brush, a maze of fallen logs, slides of broken rock and scattered aspen. It all ended at a wall of rock thirty feet high or more. An old fault line, it extended along the face of the mountain for at least half a mile.

He planned his route carefully, aiming for what seemed to be a fracture in the face of the rock, a possible way to the top without going far around the end. The crack, if that was what it was, could not be seen clearly from here; but once in the saddle he led off, weaving a precarious way through the obstacles on the mountainside.

Twice he paused, letting Mat and the pack horses go ahead, remaining behind just long enough to tumble rocks over their path that would bar any horse from following. Brionne knew that anyone tracking them would have to waste time finding his trail again, and every minute thus wasted would be an advantage to him. Somewhere ahead they were going to stop, and they would need time to find the kind of position he wanted.

Suddenly, the crack was before them. It was scarcely wide enough for a horse, and it meant a difficult scramble to the top. Brionne dismounted and led his horse, grunting and scrambling, up the steep way. He tied the horse, pausing only long enough to catch his breath, then he descended and brought Mat to the top. After that he brought up the pack horses.

Looking around, he found the fallen trunk of a long-dead pine. Getting behind it, and using a broken limb for a lever, he worked the heavy log over until he could topple it into the crack, closing it off.

They were now on a rugged plateau, which formed the top of the Uintah Range. It was a wide, uneven plateau, broken by canyons and ridges, and dotted with many lakes. There were forested slopes and open, grassy meadows. Within the space of a few minutes he saw tracks of the bighorn sheep, the mule deer, and wild horses.

The blue spruce and aspen thinned out up here, and on the ridges ahead he could see alpine fir and another type of spruce that grew in this high altitude. Everywhere there were marks of glacial action. He pointed them out to Mat, keeping up a running commentary on the country, the trees, and the tracks. All around them were snow-covered peaks.

"How high are we?" Mat asked.

"I'd guess about eight, nine thousand feet—maybe closer to nine."

He stopped to let the horses take a breather. He had gained a little time, and the ridge ahead should offer a camp with some security.

He had no idea who his enemies might be, if those who followed him were, indeed, enemies. Out here he was relatively unknown. It was unlikely that anyone else remembered, as the Ute warrior had, the young cavalry officer of a time before the War Between the States. But somehow, in some way, he must have impressed someone as being a danger, or perhaps possessing some coveted knowledge.

Did they connect him with Miranda Loften? After all, they had ridden the same train west, and they had had some small association on that train. Could they guess that he had not known her until he left his son in her care when he went to fight the fire?

His choice then had been simple. He had, on entering the car, mentally catalogued the occupants. Miranda Loften had impressed him at once with her quiet dignity, her air of gentility, and her natural sympathy. He had sensed that she liked children and would be warm and responsive to Mat. It had been as simple as that . . . but would everyone see it so?

Yet he had interfered in her affairs. He had, without asking permission, or even mentioning the fact, deliberately begun to try to solve the problem of the silver mine.

Why?

James Brionne was a reasoning man, and he asked himself this question seriously for the first time. Why, indeed? Was it simply because he needed some direction to follow? Was it because all his life he had moved from one goal to another? Always with some destination in view, always with some purpose? Or was it because of her aloneness, and the fact that he was a Virginia gentleman?

Or—and he hesitated even to frame the question—was it because she was so attractive? Because she was, in fact, a very lovely girl?

"You've read too much of Sir Walter Scott," he said aloud.

"What was that, pa?"

He looked over his shoulder. "Nothing, son. I was just talking to myself. You'll find it is a habit men acquire when they're riding in the wilderness."

"Was this where Fremont was, pa?"

There had been much talk of Fremont around their home, and Mat knew the stories of Fremont's explorations in the West, and of Kit Carson.

"Not far from here. Father Escalante traveled some of the trails we traveled a few days back. He came through here with a very small party in 1776. But I doubt if he was ever up this far into the mountains. If he was, there's nothing in his journals about it."

Suddenly he drew rein. Not thirty feet from the way they were following was a small stump showing the marks of an axe. Leaving Mat with the pack animals, Brionne walked his horse over to the stump. Then he called, "Mat . . . come here."

When the boy rode up beside him, Brionne indicated the stump. It was scarcely four inches in diameter, and it had been cut off about a foot above the ground.

"Wherever an axe has been used," he said, "the mark of the cut shows white for quite a while. Now, whoever cut that either wanted a pole or he wanted firewood. I think he wanted firewood, because he even picked up the biggest chips."

He walked his horse in a widening circle, and it took him only a few minutes to find a small lean-to and the remains of a fire. The bits of charcoal lying there had been worn smooth by rain and wind ... it was an old fire.

"Maybe this means nothing," he said to Mat, "but it might be important. I doubt if many men have come up this high, but I feel quite sure that Ed Shaw did. When we scout around a little we may find where he went."

Brionne rode around the camp in widening circles, but he found no tracks. He studied the distant ridge where the sun shone bright upon the sullen and silent rocks, and he started toward it. On this wide plateau there was no sound except the footfalls of their own mounts, and the sound of the wandering wind, a wind uncertain of itself, prowling among the trees as if looking for something lost.

Again and again Brionne drew up to look about, to listen, and to watch the trail behind. For all its beauty, there was an eerie something about this plateau that made him wary. He somehow had the feeling of eyes watching him, eyes that might be looking along a rifle barrel.

He changed course several times. He would veer

suddenly to put a bush, a tree, or a rock behind him. He was trying to offer no target for a marksman, and his sudden changes were useful in making his trail difficult to follow. Instinctively, he chose the way that would leave the fewest marks behind. For he felt that even if he was not followed now, he would be soon.

Quite suddenly, in front of them, lay a lake, its blue waters ruffled by the wind. He skirted the shore and, seeing the water was shallow, he and Mat rode in and walked their horses close to the shore for half a mile. They left the lake by a small stream that came down from the ridge toward which they had been traveling.

They made camp in the gathering dusk in a corner of the ridge, gathering dry wood from old deadfalls that would make an almost smokeless fire.

It was a good camp. The cove was higher than the land in front of it, offering a good view for perhaps a quarter of a mile. The camp itself lay in a slight hollow under fir trees that would help to spread any smoke there might be from their fire.

"We will stay here for a couple of days, Mat," Brionne said. "We need to rest the horses, and I expect you could use the rest, too. I know I could."

"I'm all right, pa," Mat answered.

After a good supper, they bedded down, the horses picketed behind them on the grass.

Just before turning in, Brionne went to a hidden lookout, which was behind some rocks and under the branches of the trees. He lay there for some time, listening to the night, then he went back to the camp. The fire was already banked, only faint coals showing red.

Seven miles away, hidden in a small grove of trees well back from the shores of a lake, Dutton Mowry squatted near the campfire. He looked across the fire at Miranda Loften. "You still game, ma'am? You begin to see what this here is like?"

"I am game," Miranda answered, and she smiled at him. And then she added, "We are not far from the mine now."

He gave her a sharp glance. "How do you figure that? You seen some landmark?"

"Yes."

"Well, I'll be forever damned." He poked a stick into the fire, and when it blazed up, lit his cigarette. "You must've had mighty good directions, or else you're mighty mistaken."

"I am not mistaken. We are close ... another day—possibly two."

Mowry looked at her with respect. She had evidently picked up more than one landmark, and had been keeping them in sight. Earlier she had expressed a wish to pass close to the lake, and as it had been a likely course, he had taken the route she suggested.

"Don't forget that rifle," he warned her now, and let his eyes sweep their campsite again. It was a good one, but he was not a trusting man, and he knew what the Allards were like. How had he ever let himself get trapped into a situation like this? With a woman to watch over, when they would have been enough by themselves?

"You ever hear of Caleb Rhodes?" he asked her suddenly.

She hesitated, letting a moment pass; then after obviously considering her reply, she said, "Yes."

"He had him a mine up here somewhere, too. Only his was gold."

"He had two mines," she corrected. "One was lode, the other placer."

"Your Uncle Rody must've told you plenty," he commented dryly.

"Where do you suppose he is?" she asked suddenly.

"Who?"

She flushed slightly, and Mowry stifled a smile. "Major Brionne . . . I mean, who else is up here?"

"Them Allards are, and Brionne doesn't know it. He doesn't know who is follerin' him." He finished his coffee, and dropped his cigarette into the coals. "I got a hunch we'll see him, and soon," he said.

He looked at her, his eyes masking the twinkle with a solemn expression. "Why don't you go ahead an' marry him? I can just see you settin' your cap for him."

"That is not true!" she said primly, but she could feel herself blushing. And it was not true; she had thought of no such thing . . . so why was she embarassed?

"Makes a lot of sense," he said, keeping his eyes serious. "You an' him. He needs him a wife, and you shouldn't be traipsin' around out here with no man to care for you. It ain't fittin'."

"I think it is time to go to sleep," she said. "I am tired."

"He'd be kind of easy to catch right now, ma'am. He's all unwary, like. He's lonesome as all get out, you can see that. An' that kid needs a woman's hand. You could sort of ease up on his blind side, make up to the kid, and first thing you know you'd have him all wrapped up and hogtied."

"Good *night,* Mr. Mowry!"

"Good night, ma'am."

After Dutton Mowry had rolled up in his blankets he lit a cigarette. Presently, looking up at the stars, he said earnestly, "He's a mighty fine figure of a man, that Brionne. Him an army man, and all. Why, ma'am, they do say General Grant sets real store by him."

Miranda Loften prepared herself for sleep. It was a ridiculous idea that Mowry had voiced. She had talked with the man only two or three times. Where could Dutton Mowry have gotten such an idea?

She heard a subdued chuckle from where Mowry lay in his blankets, and despite herself, she smiled.

It *was* a ridiculous idea—of course it was. He had scarcely noticed her, and as for the boy—he was a darling child. So quiet, so well-mannered. He . . .

She never knew when she fell asleep, nor did she hear the wind in the trees, nor smell the pines, nor glimpse the star that kept twinkling through the boughs of the tree under which she slept.

The wind was cool off the snow-covered peaks. The lake water lapped softly against the shelving beach.

Two miles to the east a huge grizzly stretched himself tall and dug his claws into the bark of the tree, drawing furrows in the bark, leaving his sign for all to see. He smelled bear, knew this was a bear tree, and had confidence in his own great size and strength. He would make his mark, a challenge for all.

Had he come along a little earlier in the day he

would have seen other claw marks, claw marks much deeper and eight inches higher up the trunk.

The wind stirred, bringing him a faint man smell, and he growled inquisitively. The wind brought an intimation of danger, but of reward also. He remembered a time, two summers ago, when he had looted a camp. He remembered the side of bacon he had eaten, and the sugar; especially the sugar.

For the moment he was not hungry, and he lumbered off up the trail toward a hollow under a fallen tree where he intended to sleep.

He paused only once, warily, for he heard a faint stir of movement in the night. Something or somebody was coming . . . more than one.

He smelled men again, and horses, and they were moving in the night.

9

During the night the wind came roaring across the dark face of the mountain, roaring through the tree tops, whining in the crevices of the rocks, and stirring small pebbles and rock fragments to start them rolling.

Mat crowded close to his father, and lay wide-eyed in the night, having never known such wind as this that moaned across the high lakes and among the peaks. He lay and trembled, but he was calmed by the stillness of his father beside him.

Overhead the great trees bent before the wind, and against the sky the ragged peaks lost themselves in the tearing clouds; they broke the clouds apart and appeared again, but vanished once more amid the rising sea of darkness.

"Pa?"

His father was awake. "It's all right, Mat. It is only a storm. The mountains do not mind the storms. There have been many storms upon these rocks."

Mat lay quiet, thinking of his father's words, wishing he could be like him, so sure and quiet. And he said as much.

"No one can be sure, Mat. But a man learns to appear that way, and after a while it is the same thing. Look to the hills, Mat. They are quiet. The storms sweep over them and are gone, and most of man's troubles pass the same way. That is one reason I brought you here, just to learn that. Whenever you feel that things are getting too much for you, go to the mountains or the desert—it smooths out the wrinkles in your mind."

After a few moments Mat spoke again.

"Pa? What happened to those men? The ones who ... who burned our house?"

"I don't know. They're probably still in the mountains ... or in Missouri."

"Could they be out here, pa? Could it be some of them who shot at you?"

Surprised, Brionne considered it. The idea had occurred to him, but only in a fleeting way. It was unlikely the Allards would leave their home mountains and their relatives. That they would come to this part of the country would be too much of a coincidence.

Yet the thought nagged at him. Many of the lawless had followed the railroad west, and when the last spike was driven at Promontory they had spilled over into the country around.

"There's not much chance of it, Mat," he said aloud. "But we'll keep our eyes open." Then after a pause he asked, "How many of them would you remember if you saw them again?"

"Two, I think. Maybe three."

The unfortunate part was that Brionne did not know them by sight. Only one or two of the family had appeared at the trial, and they were the lesser ones, unwanted by the law.

He said no more to Mat, and soon he heard the boy's even breathing, and knew that he was asleep. He slipped from under the blankets, pulled on the moccasins he always carried, and checked the horses. The cove was sheltered from the worst of the wind, and the horses seemed content.

Back in his blankets he slept, but before daybreak he was up, and made a quick breakfast. "Stay in the cove," he told Mat after they had eaten. "I may scout around a mite, but I'll be close by. We're going to rest here."

There was grass for three or four days, at least. There was good water, and their position could not be easily approached. They would simply wait. Brionne wanted to do some thinking.

Mat had put into words a vague suspicion that had been lingering almost unnoticed in the back of Brionne's mind. It had taken only the boy's suggestion to bring the idea into focus. Could it be that the Allards were out here?

At first thought it had seemed too much of a coincidence, but a bit of consideration changed that. There was only one railroad west, the Union Pacific.

The last spike of that railroad had been driven only a short time ago. It had been driven, in fact, since the death of his wife and the burning of his home.

Suppose the Allards had, after leaving their mountain country, elected to take the railroad west? They were being hunted throughout the mountains, they were being hunted in Missouri, where they had come from. If they had taken to the railroad, what more likely place for them to end up than in Promontory or Corinne?

The man in the Southern Hotel might have been one of them who alerted the others; or they might even have come west, following him. But it was more likely that the man from the hotel, on his way west to join them, had recognized Brionne. The horses in the baggage car had been there only a short time. It left questions to be answered, but there was a possibility that something of the kind had happened.

So the Allards might be here. If so, they now knew about him. Without doubt, they would not attribute his arrival here to coincidence; they would be sure he had somehow tracked them down. And they would try to kill him.

Meanwhile there was the problem of Ed Shaw's silver mine. There was a lot he did not know about Ed Shaw and about Rody Brennan. How had they come to die? Were they both actually dead? Everyone spoke of them as if they were dead, but he had no details.

If Ed Shaw had read the message of the trail from the Indian writing on the walls of Nine Mile Canyon, then he had come in from the south. Such directions could not pinpoint such a thing as a mine, so there must be some other identifying marks.

What Ed Shaw must have seen was such simple signs as those for rivers, peaks, and trails. Perhaps there was a sign for silver, or for metal. These would have taken him into the area, and from there on he, too, must have relied on local signs.

He had moved some distance from the camp when he heard a faint stir of movement behind him. It was Mat.

"I got lonesome, pa."

"Sure. Come and sit down."

They were silent together, observing the country. After a while Brionne said, "You have to learn to see country, Mat, to pick out details, and to remember them. Some of the mountain men were educated men, but some of them could neither read nor write, but they had a perfect memory for the lay of the land."

"Have you been here before, pa?"

"No . . . not right in this part of the country. But I have talked to men who have been here. I have talked to Kit Carson and to Jim Bridger . . . and to a dozen others. They knew the country and they told me what they knew, and I have not forgotten."

He had been aware for a few moments of something stirring at the edge of his vision, and he turned to look. "We have company, Mat. Don't you move. Just sit very quiet, and watch."

Two riders had emerged from the trees and were holding a trail that would bring them not far from the cove. They were riding easily, and leading some pack horses. "See anything odd about the way the second one rides, Mat?"

"Why . . . it's a lady!"

"That's right, Mat. She's riding side-saddle. I think it is your friend, Miranda Loften."

He took up his field glasses and studied them. "Dutton Mowry is with her. Now what about that?"

He watched them as they drew nearer, then as Mat started to rise, he put his hand out. "Don't move . . . let them go by."

"But they're our friends!"

"Perhaps, but let them go and we can join them later if we like."

Brionne understood the boy's disappointment. Mat had taken to that young woman as he did to few people, and he wanted to see her again. That she was honestly looking for a mine, Brionne did not doubt. About Dutton Mowry he was not so sure.

The man had loafed around Promontory, had made no effort to find a job, yet he seemed to have more cash than any drifting cowhand was likely to have. And he wore his gun well . . . too well. He wore it like a man who had used it, and who could use it fast and well. If he was not one of the new breed of gunfighters, Brionne was much mistaken.

He watched them pass, his eyes measuring their stock, their gait, trying to estimate the probable distance they would manage before sundown.

After they had gone by and Mat started to get up again, Brionne put a hand on his arm. "Not now . . . wait."

The minutes passed, and still Brionne waited. When almost half an hour had gone by, his grip on Mat's arm grew tight.

Out of the trees came several horsemen. Startled, Mat looked at his father. Had he known they were coming? His father was watching them, counting them as they emerged from the trees.

"Four . . . five . . . six," he whispered. Six men, and all well mounted; but they were so far away he could not see their faces. Their gait was leisurely. Once they drew up to talk together. Obviously they were not trying to catch up to Miranda and Mowry.

"There's trouble, Mat," Brionne said quietly. "Trouble for them and for us."

"Who are they, pa?"

"I don't know, but they are following your friend Miss Loften and Dutton Mowry. They are probably trying to locate Rody Brennan's silver mine."

"What will we do?"

"Go back to camp, cook something, and have a good meal. That's what we'll do."

After they had eaten beside their small fire, Brionne checked his weapons. He was under no illusions as to what might happen in the next few days, perhaps even within the next few hours.

He could, of course, run for it. He could leave now, going back down the mountain and out of this region, leaving Mowry and Miranda to their own doings. But this would solve nothing. The Allards would still be around, always a potential threat. The way to face trouble, he realized, was to meet it head-on.

He knew he could not leave Miranda Loften to Dutton Mowry alone. The gunfighter—if Mowry was one—seemed a tough, capable man, but Brionne knew what the Allards were capable of.

It was afternoon before he led the way out of the cove. He and Mat dropped down on the flat to check the tracks of the horses, and then started at a trot to follow them.

He knew he was taking his son into trouble, but the world in which they were living was one where there was bound to be trouble, and many a child on the frontier had grown up in Indian country, with all its dangers.

After an hour or so Brionne pulled off the trail and went ahead with greater caution. Here and there the men he was following had also slowed. Evidently Miranda Loften was less sure of her trail now, and was taking her time.

The air was cool and fresh off the snow-covered peaks. The streams, which they now encountered with greater frequency, were very cold and clear.

The old feeling was on him again, the sense not only of stillness, but of keen awareness, of expectancy. It was a feeling that belonged to the wild country, to the lonely lands. James Brionne was not, and never had been, a man for desks and cities. He had lived that life because it was in large measure the life of his time and place; but always, deep within him, there ran a tide of fierceness, a touch of the primitive.

"Keep your eyes open, Mat," he said to his son. "You might hear or see something I might miss. We are riding into trouble."

"What shall I do?"

"Watch, and learn. At your age that is all there is to do. Don't be frightened. Above all, keep out of the way. Remember who those men probably are . . . don't trust them—not for a minute."

"What about Miranda Loften and Mr. Mowry?"

"I think they are both good people, Mat, but we

do not know them well yet. Don't trust anybody too much too soon." He paused. "We are all human, and being human we can all make mistakes. There's a silver mine up there; and when there is wealth to be had, even people who know better sometimes become too greedy."

"Do they think that way about you?"

Brionne smiled. "If they don't, they should. If they knew me better they would know I am to be trusted. I never wanted wealth that much, but they do not know that. There's only one thing I want now ... I want to see you grow up to be a fine man. I am a little afraid that anyone who tried to hurt you might run into quite a bit of trouble with me. ... Now let's move on, and we must be quiet."

The peaks began to point shadows at them. They were riding northeast now and some of the ridges were already behind them. They dipped down into the forest again, and their horses walked on needles, making no sound; there was only the creak of the saddles.

Again and again Brionne drew up and paused; then suddenly he veered sharply into the trees. A lake was before them, and on the shores of the lake was a small fire.

He studied the scene through his glasses. It was Dutton Mowry and Miranda Loften who were beside the fire. It was burning quite brightly, with no shelter of any kind around. Brionne was disturbed by this. The fire was too conspicuous. It was sure to attract attention.

He started his horse, and Mat followed. They took a route that kept them well back under the trees, and went slowly in a semicircle that skirted the fire and more or less followed the lake shore. Once, because of an arm of the lake, they had to ride deep into the forest.

When they reached a place where the canyon of Rock Creek was on their right, a ridge of the mountain on their left, Brionne drew rein. "We'll wait for them here, Mat," he said.

"Who?"

"Mowry and your friend. They'll be coming along in a very short time, unless I miss my guess."

They waited . . . the air grew colder. The wind came down from the higher peaks to the north. Several times something stirred down in the canyon. Whatever it was made the horses restless. "Mountain lion," Brionne whispered to Mat, "or maybe a bear."

They heard the other faint sound before they realized they were hearing it. And then it was a gentle but definite sound that brought them sharply to awareness—the soft footfalls of walking horses.

As they came nearer, Brionne began to sing softly, *"We're tenting tonight on the old campground, give us a song to cheer . . ."*

The sounds ceased.

". . . our weary hearts, a song of home, and friends we . . ."

"A fella could get himself shot thataway." Mowry spoke in a low, conversational tone. "He surely could."

James Brionne rode out into the open. "I was waiting for you," he said, "and I thought you should have some warning before I came riding out on the trail."

"How'd you know we were comin'?"

"We saw your fire, so we figured you'd be along in a little while."

"But how did you know it was us?" Miranda questioned. "Mr. Mowry was so sure we'd fool them—those men following us."

"I think you have. They don't know Mowry here, and that's just the sort of fire a romantic girl might build. By now, they're probably safely bedded down and waiting for light."

"Romantic?" Her voice raised a little. "Why do you say I am romantic?"

Brionne smiled into the darkness. "Put it down to too much reading of Sir Walter Scott."

"We'd best move on," Mowry said dryly. "This here ain't just the place for no tea-party talk."

They rode on, with Mowry leading. Brionne asked no questions, and made no comment. Obviously the girl was either so sure of herself that she could go on in the dark, or more likely the landmarks she was going by were so obvious they could not be missed.

He dropped back until Mat was ahead of him. He knew the boy was tired, and he wanted him where he could see him—as much as anybody could be seen in such a place on such a night.

If Brionne's memory served him right, Deadhorse Pass was somewhere ahead of them, or to the east. Were they going to cross over the pass? Or was the mine on this side? If so, they were getting close.

Tomorrow ... tomorrow all hell might break loose.

10

Cotton Allard drew up and waited in the small clearing. As Hoffman, Peabody, Tuley, and the others closed around him, he indicated the trail. "They got together," he said. "Brionne, the girl and whoever's with her."

"The boy, too?"

"Of course, the boy. You figger he'd leave him somewheres on the mountain?" Cotton stared up at the peaks, not far distant now. "I never heard of no mines up this high."

He lit the stub of a cigar. "We got 'em. They ain't got a chance." He turned to a small wiry man with a patchy beard. "Cricket, you think they'll cross over?"

"I doubt it. This here leads to Deadhorse Pass, though." He stared at the peaks, then spat into the damp earth. "That girl surely knows somethin', Cot. She surely does. Now, you take the trail she's been layin' out—an' we've seen from the tracks that more'n half the time she's been the guide—she couldn't have found that trail without she had some knowledge aforehand."

"You think there really is a mine?"

"Well, she ain't just goin' for a ride. That Brennan must've told her somethin'. Or maybe he give her a map. Anyway you look at it, she's got to know somethin'. Why, long as I been in this country I couldn't have done better myself. She ain't missed a trick."

"What do we do now, Cotton?" Tuley asked.

Cotton Allard rolled the stub of the cigar in his teeth. "Why, we ride up there. We kill Brionne an' that drifter she's got wranglin' stock for her, and then we make her talk."

"What about the kid?"

Cotton shrugged. "Womenfolks are soft on kids. If she don't want to talk, maybe what we do to the kid will make her feel like it."

"I never killed a kid," Hoffman muttered. "I don't like it."

Cotton turned his cold eyes on Hoffman and stared at him until the man shifted in his saddle and the sweat broke out on his forehead.

"You been handy," Cotton said, speaking around his cigar. "You been mighty useful, knowin' about trains an' such; an' when the gold shipments start from Californy you'll be handy again. Don't you make us forget that, Hoff. I tell you what you do. When we start to work on the kid, you just go for a walk in the woods. But," he added, his icy look fixed on Hoffman, "I wouldn't go too far. We wouldn't want to figure you runnin' away now, would we?"

They started on through the forest. The trail was difficult to follow, but the problem was not one to worry about, for there was simply no place for their quarry to go but straight ahead.

The trees around them were spruce and alpine fir. Occasionally, when they rode out on some knoll, over the tops of the trees they could see the peaks and ridges above timberline. White streaks of snow showed on the bare rock, while above on the peaks themselves were the remnants of ancient glaciers, the ice and snow of many winters. Here and there a stunted fir or a lightning-struck lone tree would indicate an effort by the forest to advance beyond the limit set for it, an attempt to encroach upon the domain of the lichen and the moss.

"We'll come up with them before they get to the pass," Cricket said. "It ain't far now."

Hoffman was riding last. He was frightened. He had come from the same part of Missouri as the Allards, had known them for years, and when they found he had worked for the railroad they enlisted his help.

At first they had stolen horses belonging to the stage line. They had raided a couple of railroad cars where Hoffman had told them there would be rifles, ammunition, food, and liquor. Once he had been able to indicate where there would be a chest of silver dollars to be used in paying off some Indians.

He had told them, too, that there would be shipments of gold from the California mines, and that he could find out when the shipments were to be moved. He had used his friendship with the conductor, as well as a small cash payment, to get their horses into the baggage car, but he had bargained for nothing like this.

Killing Brionne would create a stir, but they could survive that if it happened in some out-of-the-way place. Killing a young boy and a woman ... well, that was something else again, and he did not like it. However, he was afraid of Cotton Allard.

"We'd better pull up," Cricket suggested suddenly. "We got to ride into the open up yonder, and I'd say we'd best look it over."

"You sit tight," Cotton ordered. "I'll do the lookin'."

James Brionne took a cigar from an inside pocket, bit off the end, and lighted it, and then squinting his eyes against the smoke, he looked past the match toward the way they had come. As the day had gone on he had become somber and still. Again and again he delayed to study their trail, and he felt growing within him an old fierceness, a feeling he had had only once or twice since the end of the war.

He had felt it on that awful night when he had come to find his house in flames, flames already dying down as day was coming. He had felt it during those months of search when he had thought of nothing but finding the men responsible.

Now he knew they were behind him. They were back there, coming along his trail.

Dutton Mowry had told him what he had suspected, and now once more that deep and terrible rage, never quite extinguished, was mounting within him. There was in him something of the old Viking berserker, who threw all caution to the winds and charged, blade in hand, thinking only to cut down his enemy.

Devine had known that quality was in him, and feared for him. So had Grant.

They were down there somewhere now, those men who had attacked his home, and who were responsible for his wife's death. The men who had sent his son into hiding, and who now were trailing them.

They would find him. He had already decided on that. He would find the right place somewhere farther on, and from that point he would go no further. If they wanted him, they were going to find him.

He drew slowly on the cigar. It would not be long now . . . perhaps sometime later today, or the following morning.

But he wanted them to know what was to come. He wanted no doubt about that.

Beside the trail was a flat gray slab of rock. Dismounting, he hunted around over the remains of one of the old, lightning-struck trees to find a few pieces of charcoal. When he had them he stooped over the flat rock.

After a few moments he mounted and rode on.

The men heard Cotton Allard swearing before they came up to him, and when they drew alongside they saw the slab of rock.

It was propped up, squarely in the center of the trail, and on it were the words: *I shall be waiting for you.*

Tuley stared at it uneasily. "What d'you suppose he means by that?"

"Well," Hoffman said, "he knows we're coming."

"I don't like it, Cot," Peabody said. "I don't like it none a-tall."

Cotton looked at the words written on the rock, then looked ahead at the trail. He would not have said it aloud, but he did not like it either. There was no question of surprise now. They would be ready for a fight. He scanned the rugged slopes, the jutting crags, the tumbled talus, and the slabs of fallen rock. They might be anywhere up there . . . waiting.

"What's it mean?" Tuley said again. "Where'll he be waiting? And what's he waitin' for?"

"Got to hand it to him," Peabody declared. "He sure don't sound like he's scared none."

"There's nothin' up there but two men, a girl, an' a kid," Cotton stated matter-of-factly. "An' they ain't goin' much further."

"That's a mighty tough man up there," Hoffman said. "He was an Indian fighter before the war, they say."

"You scared?" Peabody sneered at him. "He won't have no more chance than a treed 'coon."

Cotton looked again at the sign. "All right," he said. "Let's go get him!"

They started on, holding to what cover the trail offered. They rode with caution now, their seeking eyes uneasy upon the slope. It was one thing to be following a group they expected to ambush or capture when the time was right; quite another to have one or more of that group lying up there in the rocks watching for them with a rifle.

Hoffman's horse was lagging. Hoffman had no

stomach for this. He had never fancied himself a fighting man, although he had, like most western men, had a few brushes with Indians. There was nothing about his memory of James Brionne that gave him any feeling of security.

They were strung out single file. They could see what seemed to be a zigzag trail toward the top of the pass.

The sign bothered Cotton. Why would a man do a thing like that? Why take time to stop and write that notice? It made no kind of sense.

The thought nagged at him and worried him. He himself would never have done such a thing, and it disturbed him that Brionne had ... there must be something behind it.

He glanced up at the cliffs. There were plenty of places up there where a man might hide, and a good man with a rifle would be hard to get at.

But no shot came. The trail grew steeper, and somewhat more narrow. Now they could not see what was above them, but in front of them the trail dropped steeply as they dipped into a hollow. Off to their right the slope fell away, too abruptly for a man to negotiate on a horse.

Only two miles further along, Miranda Loften had pulled up short. The landmarks given her by Rody Brennan, who had them from Ed Shaw, had failed her for the first time.

Until now they had been easy to find ... obvious in a country of many lakes, many peaks, many spots that could be used to indicate a route. But the canyons that cut through the plateau had restricted the possible ways they could go.

Mowry came up beside her while James Brionne turned his horse to watch down the mountain behind them. From where they sat their view covered a wide stretch of open country, but on the gray, white streaked slope below, clear to the edge of the trees, nothing moved. Of course, there were places along the trail that were hidden from view. He considered the situation, and liked none of it.

This delay would allow the Allards to gain ground, and he was not yet ready to make a stand. First, he wanted to get Miranda and Mat into a safe place where they would be out of range of any gunfire.

The mine had to be close by, if there was a mine. He was quite sure that, given time, he could find it. In the first place, Shaw's directions had been explicit. Without them, it was unlikely the mine could be found. And it would be like Shaw to be explicit in somehow marking the mine.

Brionne suddenly thought he saw, far below on the slope, something stir, then immediately vanish.

"Major," Mowry said just then, "Miss Loften's run out of trail. We got to have time to look around."

"There's a lake just below the pass," Miranda said, "a small lake with some rock walls on its shore line. There are springs flowing down one of those walls. The springs make quite a bit of mist, falling as they do. There's a place in there to camp."

They moved on, Mowry in the lead, and Miranda fell back near Mat. The girl certainly could ride, Mowry thought, and she had not complained even once at what had been a rough, grinding trip.

Brionne let them ride ahead, then noticed something on the rock wall alongside the trail that set him smiling.

A fallen log had wedged itself so that it lay crossways, held in place only by a small rock. Behind and above the log was a great pile of debris of broken rock and slabs, a pile amounting to several tons. Working with care, Brionne took a dead limb from one of the stunted trees and placed it across the trail by the log in such a way that if it was lifted the log would shift and the whole mass would come toppling down. It took only a few minutes, and then he rode on after the others.

The dip in the trail had taken them back into the timber, but now the trail began to leave the trees behind. Twice Brionne stopped to prepare possible traps.

His first one, using the rock slide, could kill a man if he tried to move the tree limb without looking the situation over. It could even kill the whole lot of them. The other "traps" were merely tricks to slow up the pursuit and make the pursuers more wary.

When they reached the lake they found that it was closed in between two rocky cliffs. The air was damp with mist from the springs, but there was a ready and easy water supply for themselves and their horses.

At a corner of the rocks Brionne found the perfect hide-out, a small glade unapproachable from above and offering only one approach on the level. This space was littered with boulders, too small to afford hiding places, but too big to charge through on horseback. There was a good field of fire, and excellent cover.

Behind the glade a narrow crack in the rock wall

gave access to a sand-floored shelter under the rock wall that could have stabled twenty horses. There was access, too, to the springs by a narrow footpath, and there seemed to be a vague trail up through the rocks toward the pass.

They saw the remains of old campfires, some where the charcoal was worn smooth by time; but one fire must have burned only a few weeks or at most a couple of months before.

Stripping the riding saddles and pack saddles from the horses, they turned them out on the sand-floored semicavern and let them find their way to the lake for water. Meanwhile, Brionne moved a few rocks near the opening, building the wall higher, and closing a few gaps.

He was cool and methodical now. Their trouble was upon them, and there was no avoiding it, nor did he wish to. This was the conclusion he had expected would come, and for which he had hoped.

"Mat, you stay close to Miranda," he said to his son. He had called her by her first name without even realizing it. She looked at him quickly, but his mind was on other things. "Stay with her," he repeated, "and both of you keep back under the overhang and out of sight."

Miranda Loften had opened the packs and was getting out some food. Mowry had put wood together for a fire, but there was little fuel. Some of the wood he used had been carried here by earlier travelers, and some he picked up along the slope where the forest played out.

"I think your mine is somewhere close," Brionne said to Miranda, "and I think Ed Shaw left some sort of a marker for Rody Brennan. Evidently he feared something might happen ... and to a man traveling alone in this kind of country almost any accident could prove fatal. And he was all alone ... miles from any help."

"Likely he never expected any help," Mowry said. "Like us."

Brionne went out to the rocks and Miranda brought him his coffee there and a sandwich made of a chunk of beef and the last of their bread. She lingered beside him as he ate, watching the trail.

"What was she like?" she asked. "Your wife, I mean."

His eyes swept the country before them, searching every nook and cranny with the practiced eye of the skilled observer. Passing quickly here, lingering there, noting almost unconsciously every change of color and shade, every movement, every stir of dust.

"She was tall, clean-limbed—an aristocrat in the best sense of the word. She had humor and she had style. Before that night"—he paused a moment— "before the night she was killed, or killed herself, she had never faced any real emergency, but her breed always knew how to act at such a time.

"Those men were forcing their way into *her* home, and she had no intention of permitting it. She told her son where to hide, and then she waited for them.

"The fire destroyed the house, but the least damage was done right where she was. Obviously she had waited in a chair on the landing for them. It gave her the best view of the front hall.

"Evidently she got one of them. We found an exploded shell in the shotgun. And then as they rushed her she must have deliberately shot herself."

"She was very brave," Miranda said quietly.

"Yes, she was. But she would not have considered it bravery. It was simply what had to be done. One did not permit strangers to come bursting into one's home that way. One did not submit to violence to oneself or to one's home.

"And as I said, she had style. She had wit, humor, and brains."

"She would be hard to follow," Miranda said.

"No one should ever 'follow' anyone else; no one takes the place of another, and in the best sense, no one ever does. Each one blazes his or her own trail."

They were silent, and Brionne watched below. There was no movement, but he had not expected there would be. The Allards would be doing their own surmising, and would expect him to be somewhere up on the slope, waiting. They were cautious men, dangerous fighters, and they would use their heads now.

Oddly enough, he felt neither apprehension, nor the tense suspense of waiting. Inwardly a great stillness filled him, a quietness such as he had not known in a long time. He was empty of feeling in that moment—he was simply waiting for what he knew must come.

He had no preconceived plan, for he had no idea of how or when they might attack. His mind was open, his senses were exposed. He had no feeling— he was only seeing, hearing . . . he was ready.

Miranda Loften sat near him, and he was conscious that he liked her being there. She did not speak, and he was glad of her silence. She was a sensitive person, aware of feelings; her sensitiveness went outward, a subtle awareness of the feelings of others.

The cool wind from over the pass touched them, and she shivered. After a long time she said, "What is going to happen?"

"There will be fighting," he answered, "and some men will die."

"Doesn't that depress you?"

"No. We are naked and alone here in the West. We have no law to protect us—only scattered and limited governments in the towns or the territories. The strong have come here because it is a place for the strong; but all of the strong are not good men, and if we are to survive, if we are to become a land of homes and people, evil men must not be allowed to persist in their evil.

"Such men as the Allards, or whatever their name is, are a blight upon the land. They are like mad dogs, or like weasels. Their instinct is to do violence, to kill. Some of the bad men will change, they will learn, they will grow up with the country. Not such men as these. These will end, snarling and biting, tearing even at each other if there is no one else."

Dutton Mowry walked out to join them. "Mat's with the horses," he said. His eyes swept the mountainside. "You got any ideas, Major?"

"No. I'm just ready. The only thing I do not expect is a frontal attack. They might come tonight, but I rather think it will be tomorrow, just before daylight."

"Is it true that the Allards rode with Bloody Bill Anderson?" Mowry inquired.

"Yes. Later they organized their own outfit. They were too bloody and undisciplined even for him."

Brionne returned to the fire with Miranda and Mowry stayed on watch. Mat was curled up on a blanket near the fire, fast asleep. "He's had a rough time," Brionne said, "but he's coming through in fine shape. You know, you are the first person he's warmed up to since . . . since he lost his mother."

"He's a lovable boy."

She glanced around at the lake and the cliffs. The surroundings were growing somber with the changing hours. "I wish I could be here when there was no trouble," Miranda said. "I love it here."

He nodded. The cliffs had changed in appearance, and rose now from the steel of the gray water in the rusted iron of their sheer rock. The evening was still, and already here the night was coming, although the sky above was still clear and blue, only traced by faint streaks of rose left from the declining sun.

"One lives with trouble," Brionne said. "There is no need to think about a time without it, for it is always here. A man grows strong by standing against the wind, and eternal peace would bring no happiness. Man needs strife of some kind, something to struggle against. Although that struggle need not be with other men."

But he was feeling strangely at peace in this place, talking with this girl, and it was not the right way to feel at this moment. At any other time he would have welcomed this feeling, but now he needed that sense of awareness that he had been feeling earlier. He needed it because he knew only too well the danger they faced.

These men who were their enemies were degenerate, evil. He had known, long before it became his job to hunt down and capture the man who called himself Dave Allard, the kind of men these were. Outlaws and thieves before the war, they had taken advantage of the protective coloration it provided to release all their lust for rapine, killing, and destruction.

There was something twisted and malformed about them—perhaps nothing that was outwardly visible, but something that lurked in their minds. Yet they were woodsmen—they were men at home in the wilderness, men who knew its ways and how to use those ways. They were wily and cunning, and they were not cowards in the physical sense.

Of Cotton Allard he had heard much. The man's physical reactions were amazing, as was his muscular strength. Tuley was slower to act, but he was physically strong, and as easy on his feet as a big cat. All this Brionne had read in the record or had been told by those who knew them. During the search for Dave, and later the quest for the ones who had burned his home, he had made many inquiries, piecing the story together, bit by bit.

Now, from this moment on, it would be a fight for survival, a bitter, desperate fight in which the only way to live was to kill.

"Why did you come here?" Miranda asked suddenly.

"The boy and I were headed south, actually. We wanted a wild place where we had to keep busy every moment to live. I wanted that for both of us. We needed it to recover mentally from what had happened, and then we needed the sky, the high mountains, the good air.

"But then I thought about you. It is not easy to be alone, and to be a woman with no home, no money.

I know something of the mountains and I thought I might help, so we came over here into the Uintahs."

Mowry came down from the rocks. "Brionne? You'd better come up here. I think we're in trouble."

Brionne looked at Miranda. "Have you got a pistol?"

"Yes."

"Keep it with you ... and remember, these men are not to be trusted, not for a moment, no matter what they say, or how they act."

She watched him walk away, a tall, straight, easy-moving man, the rifle in his hand almost an extension of himself.

Then she sat down close to Mat, and waited.

11

Dutton Mowry was crouched among the scattered boulders. Only the sky above held some light; below all was darkness, and for the moment, silence.

"There ain't no way to keep watch," Mowry whispered, "and we daren't move about much up here or we'll sky-line ourselves. They'll be comin' at us out of the dark."

It was true, of course, Brionne reflected, but they dared not pull back, for that would leave their enemies in possession of the boulders. From the shelter of the rocks they could fire upon anyone near the lake shore.

"Go get some sleep," he suggested. "You'll be needing it."

When Mowry had moved back, Brionne deliberately turned his back on the valley, trusting to his ears. He studied the lay of the lake, and the pass, which was undoubtedly guarded by now, as was any route they might take that would enable them to get away.

The lake had received the melting snows, and its entire basin was filled. Swimming in its water was out of the question, for it was icy cold.

The more he considered the situation the more he resented it. He had come to this region to live quietly with his son. Mowry had come here to help Miranda discover her mine. They had been followed to this place by the Allard outfit, who had every intention of wiping them out.

James Brionne had never been much inclined to run. His theory of fighting had always been to attack. If you had twenty men, ten men, one man ... attack. There was always a way.

And the time was now ... or very soon.

He wanted the Allards, so why wait for them to come to him? Why not carry the fight to them instead? The attacker has one advantage—he can choose the time for the fight.

No sound came from below. The Allards, secure in the knowledge that Brionne and his party were trapped, were undoubtedly sleeping.

"All right," Brionne told himself, "let them sleep for now."

When an hour had gone by, he went down to the camp and woke Mowry. Briefly, he explained what he intended to do.

Dutton Mowry stared at him, and spat. "Brionne, you're a damn fool. You'll get killed sure as shootin'."

"I don't think so. Anyway, I have never liked to let the other man move first."

"It's your skin."

"I'll see you later."

Brionne did not walk toward the rocks, but toward the cliff itself; then in the deeper shadows he went quickly along until he reached the end of the cliff. The mountain fell away before him, and somewhere down there were the Allards.

He was wearing his moccasins, and he moved like a ghost, careful to put each foot down with care, trying to avoid loose rocks, easing every movment. He knew well how sound can carry on such a night, in such clear air.

He knew, too, the chance he was taking, but he believed that the very unexpectedness of it might make it work. If they waited for Cotton Allard to make the first move, they would almost certainly be caught.

When he had gone fifty yards down the slope, he squatted among the rocks and listened.

He heard nothing . . . simply nothing at all.

After a few minutes he worked his way down through the rocks. Now he could smell the smoke of a fire; but creeping and crawling as he must do, he took at least fifteen or twenty minutes to get to it.

It was in a small hollow among the rocks, right at the edge of the trees. It was a dying fire, gray ashes with a few smoldering coals and partly burned sticks.

The Allards were gone!

Crouching, rifle in hand, he lowered one knee to

the ground and considered. They had moved out, and by this time they were in a position to attack the camp and seize whoever was there. To go charging up there would only be to get himself killed, and as he had heard no shooting, it was likely they had not yet begun an attack.

To act hastily was usually to act foolishly. He must trust Mowry.

There are more ways of fighting a battle than with a gun, and it was of that he was thinking now. This had been the Allards' camp ... where were their horses? Their gear?

In the light of the still glowing coals, he could see the sand around the campfire had been disturbed by much moving about, and most of the tracks seemed to go away from the fire toward a space between two boulders.

Moving with the utmost care, in case someone had been left behind, he worked his way around the camp. Occasionally he felt of the sand before him with gentle fingers, and he managed to get on the trail they had taken into the trees. He had not gone far when he heard a horse stamp and blow.

A few minutes later he found the horses had been left alone. And their food, their clothing, their cooking pots, as well as their horses, all were here. Working swiftly, he put pack saddles on three of the horses and loaded everything. In all this time there was no sound from above.

Then he saddled one of the remaining horses, and was just about to mount when he heard a faint movement of someone coming through the trees.

Rifle in hand, he turned to face the sound.

Suddenly, the man stopped. "Hoffman? Is that you?"

"You can drop your gunbelt, my friend—or you can die."

The movement was swift. Brionne heard a hand slap leather, heard the whisper of the gun on leather as it drew, and even as he heard the sound he had his rifle in his hands out in front of him and belt-high. He squeezed off a shot.

He heard the ugly chunk of the bullet as it hit the man's belly, a sound almost lost in the blast of his enemy's pistol as it went off, shooting into the sand.

Sand stung Brionne's face, and he moved quickly, crouching lower . . . waiting.

At first he heard no other sound, then came a low moan. The man spoke, and his voice sounded surprisingly normal. "They'll get you. You ain't got a chance."

"Are you an Allard?"

"No, but I'm kin of their'n. You hit me low down, mister, low down an' hard. You goin' to strike a light?"

"And have your friends kill me? Not a chance!"

Brionne could hear the man's heavy breathing. Once it caught, and for a moment he believed the man had died, then the breathing resumed, but with a ragged, tearing sound.

"By now they've got your kid," the man said. His voice was hoarse now, and weaker.

"I don't think so. There's a good man up there with him, a mighty good man. He's from down Texas way."

"The hell you say! Not Dut Mowry?"

"You know him?"

"He's huntin' me. Leastways I'm one of them he's after. You can tell him he can tear up that reward poster. 'Cause you've just killed Tardy Benton."

James Brionne was listening. Would somebody come down to investigate? He listened for a time, but there was no sound. They might think it a trap. Still, all their outfit was here.

The thought struck him suddenly. He was not alone with Benton—there was another man here! Benton was trying to keep him talking until the man, wherever he was, could get into position.

Tardy Benton spoke again. "You still there?"

"Who's out there, Tardy?" Brionne whispered the words. "I don't want to kill anybody but Allards."

"You ain't got a chance."

"How did you come to tie up with them?" Brionne asked.

His every sense was alert. He thought the man would come close before shooting. He lifted one foot and moved it out to one side, ever so quietly.

"Rode with 'em a time or two. . . . Friend o' their'n down to Corinne got me to fetch grub to 'em. . . . Promised I could get in on the fun."

"Well, you did."

"Hell, I was broke, anyway—blew ever' dollar down to Corinne. . . . An' who lives forever?" Benton was having some difficulty getting the words out. "How much time you got? Long enough to hear your woman screamin', or your kid?" After a pause he added, "That there Cotton Allard, he's a mean one."

The voice was very weak; every word came with an effort, but Tardy Benton was game, and he wanted his killer dead. He wanted to keep him talking.

Behind them one of the horses blew faintly, as though alarmed. James Brionne rolled his weight over to the other leg, then stretched it out after bringing the second leg under him. In this way he moved closer to the dying man, and eight or nine feet from where he had been.

He was about to move again when he heard faint breathing close by, then actually felt the warmth of a breath. He swung with the butt of his rifle, but he was off balance and went sprawling as the gun roared right in his ear. He went down on top of rocks, rolled over, and swung his rifle for a shot.

The gun blasted again and the bullet spat sand within inches of Brionne's head. He fired, missed, and worked the lever on his rifle as another bullet hit close to him. This one burned his cheek.

The man loomed up, right over him, and Brionne jabbed the rifle barrel into his belly. The man grabbed the end of the barrel, trying to force it up, and Brionne pulled the trigger.

The dart of red flame illumined for one flashing instant the staring eyes, the livid face, and then the man fell face down on top of Brionne.

Brionne felt blood on his own face and thrust the man aside. He sprang up, and another gun blasted, but the shot went wide by several feet.

"You got a fool's own luck," Tardy Benton said clearly. "The third time's the charm. ... You'll get it."

Brionne wiped the blood from his face. He felt for his cartridge belt and returned a couple to his rifle. Then he tied the lead ropes of the pack horses to his saddle horn, and started off through the night, driving the spare horses ahead of him.

He found the trail up which they had come. He had a good memory for trails, and for the country over which they traveled. He remembered a place where there was a hollow, a small meadow among the trees. He found this, took the horses around a clump of screening trees and into the meadow. He stowed the food and ammunition under some brush, and picketed the horses.

Tardy Benton had come up the mountain with supplies for the Allards. He might have come alone, although that seemed unlikely with conditions what they were. So the Allards might have been reinforced.

But where had they gone? They must be somewhere up on the mountain, but as yet there had been no shot from the lake camp. Had Dut Mowry been surprised and killed or captured? And what about Mat and Miranda?

Returning to the trail, Brionne started back up the mountain. The warmth of the day had vanished before the cool wind, and now it was cold. But he dared not move fast, for his enemies might be anywhere along the trail.

He was avoiding the area of the Allard camp. He had only one idea now—to get back to the lake and discover what had happened.

How long had he been gone, he wondered, An hour? Two? He would have liked to look at his watch, but there was no light, and he dared not strike a match.

His moccasins made no sound on the trail. He moved swiftly and easily, with occasional stops to listen and catch his breath, for the altitude made climbing difficult.

When he came to the edge of the boulders again, and could look across the gravel and sand toward the lake, he saw no fire; there was no sound, there was no movement. The lake lay like a strip of steel in the dimness; all else was dark.

His mouth dry, his heart pounding, he lay watching the lake, but after several minutes he knew he was alone. There was nobody over there, nothing.

Nearing the rock wall, he worked his way back to where the horses had been sheltered. The horses were gone; the packs were gone. There was no sign of his son, of Miranda or Dutton Mowry.

Had Mowry sold them out? Was he, after all, one of the Allard gang?

There had been no shots, of that he was sure. He had not at any time been so far away that he would have missed hearing a shot. There was no evidence here of a struggle. The sand was white, and he could see the tracks of horses and people—their own tracks.

He stood alone in the night, and despite the cold he felt the sweat break out on his brow.

It must mean that they had Mat. The Allards had Mat, and they had Miranda.

He had been a fool to leave . . . a fool.

12

There was no blood anywhere on the sand. He felt sure he could have seen it on the white sand if there had been. No blood ... no shots ... so there probably had been no fight.

What did it mean? They had been surrendered to the Allards by Mowry, who had turned traitor. They had been captured somehow, without a chance to fight. Or—and this seemed the most unlikely of all— they had had some warning of the approach of the Allards, and had gotten away.

Gotten away ... how? Or if captured, where had they been taken?

Brionne had been holding himself back in the

darkness all this time, thinking. There was no panic in him. His military conditioning had taken all that out of him. Now he thought clearly, trying to isolate each fact.

He could find no signs even of a scuffle. It was possible that he might not find them in the dark, but such a scuffle would have resulted in deep indentations in the sand, the marks made by struggling men.

Mowry had not been in this country before. He might have been lying, but his actions on the trail showed no indication of previous knowledge. Had Miranda remembered something? Or had she been holding back some secret information? Perhaps she had recognized something unclear to her before.

There seemed to be nothing to do but wait. Yet even as he considered it, he knew that this was perhaps the worst place to wait. The Allards, if they did not have Mat and the others, might come back here to look for them, or for him. On the white sand any movement of his could be too easily seen.

After taking a long drink at one of the springs, Brionne slipped out of the cul-de-sac at the lake, went around the rocks, and climbed toward the pass.

This was a broken ridge, its sides made smooth in some places by slides, and heaped with scattered boulders or talus in others. Here the forces of erosion were always at work—wind, cold, heat, snow, ice, and rain.

Finally, near the top of the ridge, under a tilted slab of rock, he found a hiding place and shelter from the wind. He squirmed his way into the moss and broken rock, and curling up for warmth, he went to sleep.

It was dawn when he awakened.

The cold gray of morning under gray clouds found him haunted with fear for Mat and Miranda. He crouched under the slab of rock, feeling the dampness of the clouds that swirled about the higher peaks. A damp chill pervaded him, and there was something in the air that frightened him. He emerged slowly, like an animal from its den, studying all around him. Only when he was sure that nothing lay in wait for him did he begin his search for tracks.

He was not a man to whom anger came quickly; rather, it grew within him until suddenly he was swept by those black rages, rages of which he was aware and which he struggled to keep within bounds. Deliberately, he forced himself now to stand still, to breathe deeply, to fight down the thing that was rising within him.

He must keep his mind clear, or all was lost. It was only by thinking clearly that he could win. He told himself this again and again.

The Allards must also be hunting for him. Two of their men had been killed, and by now they must know their horses and outfits were gone.

That feeling in the air that he did not like he now realized was a developing storm. Now he knew that he had two antagonists—there were the Allards, whom he had to find, and there was the storm. But it was possible that the storm might prove an ally.

Mat and Miranda ... it was what had happened to them that was important. For the moment he was not considering Dutton Mowry. They had gone somewhere, and it was up to him to find them, and quickly.

He went out on the mountain and began casting for sign. It was a slow, painstaking search. There were several areas of flat rock over which they might have been taken, and at first he found nothing.

He stood, a bleak and lonely man with the cloud-fog swirling about him, looking over the face of the slide rock, the smooth face with jagged edges like frozen gray flames. This was another world. Paris and New York, Washington and Virginia did not exist for him now. This was a primeval world, and he felt as if he had become a primeval man. His son had been taken from him, his only son; and the girl . . . what was she to him? He did not face that. She had been in his care, and that was enough.

This was no land for the niceties of civilization. He was alone, and he was facing, as all primitive men had sometime faced, the horror of unreason, of men who kill without passion, or kill with hatred for those who use their mind in a better way.

Patiently, steadily, he worked back and forth across the mountain. Had they gone directly down he would have heard them. They must have gone along the side of the mountain, or up it.

He found their tracks suddenly.

There was no single track that he could make out—only a tight bunch of tracks, mingled with one another, and tramped over by those following.

He went on, his rifle in his hand, every sense alert, his movements shrouded by the thickening, darkening cloud. The air prickled with electricity. He felt it in his hair when he took off his hat to run his fingers through his hair, a way he had sometimes when thinking intently.

A black, shattered cliff towered on his left, the

mountain fell away in a steep slide to the timberline below, and there he could see a gray wall of long dead trees, some still standing, some tumbled about, limbs spread out as if in groping, or flung up starkly to the sky, tree trunks like the mummified bodies of some ancient battlefield. A slide had killed them, or a stroke of lightning, leaping along the mountain, ricocheting from peak to peak, cliff-face to boulder to tree.

As he looked, a bullet smashed rock, stinging his cheeks with fragments, and he half-turned, crouched like an animal at bay, and fired at the flash, a flash scarcely seen.

Then he ran forward three quick steps and threw the rifle to his shoulder and fired again at the running figure. The man fell, not hit, but losing his footing upon the loose rocks. He scrambled up, glancing over his shoulder in horror, as if looking for the bullet that might take him between the shoulders. But Brionne missed again, and for a second time the frantic runner slipped among the rocks. Then, scrambling desperately, he plunged through an opening and was out of sight.

Brionne was gasping for breath in the thin air. Drifting cloud cut him off from his surroundings, and he was lost in the chill depths of the fog.

It was a danger, that. He could come upon them without even realizing it.

He had noticed a crevice in the rock face on his left before the fog closed down, and he went to it now and clambered up, as quietly as possible. Every foot brought a wrenching gasp from him. His lungs fought for air, and when only a few feet up he had to stop, cling to the rocks, and rest.

They were somewhere ahead of him. Had the man at whom he fired been a straggler? And how many of them were there?

Crawling out on the flat top of the rock, he lay still, breathing hoarsely, but trying to listen. The man at whom he had fired had been trying to get to some spot in the rocks up ahead. Were the Allards there? If so, they knew he was close by. There was no surprising them. . . .

Yet why not? They would not expect a lone man to attack their camp. They would expect him to lie out and try to pick them off, one by one . . . or else to run for help.

But there was no help.

When his breath was back to normal, Brionne reloaded his rifle. Then, getting to his feet, he moved swiftly and silently along the top of the rock.

Somewhere ahead of him he heard a faint sound, a whisper, and then it was gone. Was there somebody ahead of him, moving along the rock? After a moment, he went on, holding his rifle ready in his hands.

The rock ledge along which he moved was damp and slippery, but the moccasins enabled Brionne to move easily on the wet surface, and with almost no sound. The heavy clouds, growing thicker by the minute, cut visibility to only a few feet; rarely could he see a few yards in any direction.

It was an eerie feeling, a feeling of being lost in some strange, misty world. At any step one might encounter a precipice or an enemy. After every few steps Brionne paused to listen . . . and again he heard the whispering sound.

Something was moving along the same ledge where he himself moved.

A person? A mountain lion? A grizzly? To encounter any one of them in this place would mean a fight to the death.

However, this was above the haunts of the lions; among these lonely peaks the eagles flew, and the bighorns moved among the crags. Here, except for the occasional storms, was a place of silence, broken only by the rattle of a pebble, the slide of rock, the groaning of a glacier.

Now the day was still. The clouds covered the mountain far below the place where Brionne walked, and here there was only the penetrating dampness and chill.

Had they managed to keep their packs, he wondered. Was Mat warm enough? The boy's health was good, but this damp cold, at this altitude . . .

Again he heard the faint sound, like the sliding of rough cloth on rock. He stood still for a moment, his rifle easy in his hands, ready to turn quickly in any direction.

Moving on, he found the shelf ended in a cataract of rocks that disappeared into the cloud below . . . how far? He waited there, listening again. In the thickness of the mist, all sounds would be distorted, and he could not be sure of their direction.

Brionne stood on the rim like a man standing on the far black edge of the world, and he looked down.

He knew that the stones would rattle if he started down the slide, and they would carry a warning to anyone below or beyond. He must find a way around.

To the right was the cliff face ... there was nothing there but a vast emptiness. He turned left and walked on cat feet, his ears pricked for the sound of movement.

He was a hunter, alert for those other hunters, and something in him had changed, some ancient feeling had welled up within him. He squatted down close to the rock. It was smooth except where cut by the slow passing of a glacier that had left grooves into which he could lay a finger.

He thought he heard the whispering, rough sound again—or was it the wind? He waited, thinking of his enemies somewhere around him, and only the girl and his son who were friendly to him. He heard the sound again, and now he thought it was like something creeping toward him, and was tempted to shoot ... but only a fool shoots at what he cannot see.

A mile away, huddled near a spring, Cotton Allard looked at his empty coffee cup. He knew they were waiting for him to decide, and he did not know what to say. Never in his life had he wished so much to kill a man as he wished to kill James Brionne now.

He hated Brionne because he had hunted down his brother, and he hated him because he had possessed such a home as he had seen in Virginia, and such a woman as the one who had so calmly waited for him. She would not leave his mind, tormenting him with her calmness. It nagged at him that she had bested him. She had killed one of his men, narrowly missed another shot, and then had calmly killed herself before he could put his hands on her.

He had seen the contempt in her eyes, and the memory would not leave him.

If he could kill the boy and the husband, she might be beaten then. He looked again at the empty cup, swore savagely, and filled it once more. The coffee was bitter.

Tuley spoke at last. "What are we a-goin' to do, Cotton? Just set here? That man's yonder in the mountains. So are the rest of them. As for that white-headed cow-puncher, I figure I nailed him."

"You figure!" Cotton glared at him. "That there puncher you talk about is Dut Mowry! His kind don't die easy. What I want to know is what happened to Tardy? He wasn't exactly no pilgrim. He was a fair hand with a gun."

"He's probably waiting till the fog lifts," Hoffman said hesitantly. "He couldn't find us in all this."

Cotton looked up. "Are you sure that was Brionne who shot at you? Not Mowry?"

Hoffman looked worried. He wanted to give the right answer, and was afraid he might give the wrong one. "I thought it was Brionne. I didn't get a good look at him."

Cotton Allard threw the coffee into the fire and got up. "So we don't know. Maybe he's alive, maybe he's dead."

"If we get the woman," Peabody said suddenly, "the woman an' the kid, then he's got to come to us. Besides, it'd be mighty comfortin' to have a woman around."

Cotton did not reply. He was cold. He had been cold and wet ever since he came up on the mountain, it seemed, but this was a deeper cold . . . was it fear?

The question angered him. He would have struck anyone who asked such a question ... had anyone dared.

No, it was not fear. It was just this damned country, the whole situation ... and it was the memory of that woman. There was no way to get at her. She was dead, gone. Only she was not gone, for she lived in his mind and he could still see her sitting there, looking at him so calmly, looking at those intruders into her quiet, well-kept home.

At no time had she raised her voice, at no time had she recognized them as anything but a disagreeable intrusion ... or so it had seemed to him.

"Look at it this way," Cotton said, and there was a roughness in his voice, a forced assertiveness not usually present. "They've split up. Maybe both of 'em are shot up some, maybe just one.

"We got their horses an' they ain't goin' nowheres without them. We just wait until this fog lifts, then we go get 'em."

"Cotton," Hoffman suggested tentatively, "this isn't just fog. We're away up in the mountains and these are clouds. I think they're storm clouds."

"So?" Peabody asked.

"Have you ever been this high up in a bad thunderstorm? Or suppose it snows? My advice would be—"

"Nobody asked your advice." Cotton spoke in a mean tone.

Peabody glanced at his brother, and walking over to his blankets, he lay down with his face to the rock wall. Cotton was in a mood, and Peabody knew from of old how treacherous he could become. ...

And it was worse now. Ever since they burned

that house. A body would think killing a woman was something new for him.

Tuley fed fuel into the fire and walked over to the edge of the hollow to listen.

He did not like these mountains. He would have preferred to be down among the trees, which in some places were only a few hundred feet below them. And he had a sneaking feeling Hoffman was right about the clouds.

Tuley was no more than sixty feet from the fire, standing alone, looking down the mountain when James Brionne appeared.

He did not come walking up, making sounds as he came; it just seemed that some of the fog or cloud drifted away and there he stood, like a ghost, with a rifle in his hands.

"Where is she? Where's the boy?"

His voice was low, and unconsciously Tuley Allard replied in the same tone. "I don't know. We got their outfit, but they got away from us."

"Were you there when my wife was killed?"

"Yeah, I was there. On'y she killed herself. Had herself a derringer we never seen. She killed one of us with the shotgun, then missed with the derringer, and before we could lay hold of her she shot herself."

The rifle muzzle was down. Tuley smiled, showing his broken teeth. "Cotton is goin' to be fit to be tied when he finds I've killed you."

"Tuley?" It was Cotton's voice. "Who you talkin' to?"

"Brionne;" Tuley said, "an' I'm goin' to kill him."

Tuley was a fast hand with a gun. Not so fast as Cotton, but he was an excellent shot along with his speed. He was very confident now. No ghosts disturbed his stolid, somewhat stupid temperament. His hand moved down and back. It was an easy draw. Tuley was smiling when his palm slapped the gun butt, and when the gun started to lift. He was still smiling when the rifle bullet struck his belt buckle's corner, mushroomed, and tore into his stomach.

And he still smiled as his gun was coming up, only he was on his knees and a queer numbness gripped him. His fingers no longer felt the gun's weight.

The bullet had ripped a wide gash in the wall of his stomach, glanced off a rib, and struck his spinal cord, coming to rest there.

At the first bellow of the shot, Cotton Allard hit the ground rolling and came up, gun in hand. Only there was no target. And the fire, a moment before the center of the small group, was suddenly deserted.

Cloud had drifted across the scene, swallowing it up and blotting it out. They could see nothing. Even Tuley, on his knees, eyes glazing, stared wonderingly at the place where Brionne had stood. There was only cloud. Nothing more.

Brionne, expecting fire from the camp, had dropped to his knee, and had then taken off to the right in a crouching run.

Suddenly, from farther to the right, in the vicinity of the peak, there was a brilliant flash. Brionne's skin prickled with the electricity and his hair stood on end. A moment later there was a deafening crash of thunder. Dropping his rifle, he rolled away from it, and lay in the depression between two boulders.

The cloud swirled with a sudden gust of wind; and looking up, Brionne found himself staring at a crudely drawn picture of a running dog. The picture had been scratched on the rock wall, pointing toward the right and toward the ridge.

Driven by a sudden urge, he caught up his rifle and went in the direction the dog's nose pointed. Indians sometimes used such picture devices; but this was, he felt sure, no Indian drawing. He had heard of prospectors using such markings; and somewhere near, he was convinced, was the place toward which Rody Brennan had been directed by Ed Shaw.

Farther along on the ridge, he found another crude drawing of a dog, pointing south. The ridge led him on, and the one place Brionne wanted to be now was off that ridge. He wanted to be on lower ground, where lightning was less apt to strike.

When he had traveled perhaps half a mile he found another drawing, but this time it was of a horse; and a little farther along there was one of an Indian with a bow, about to release an arrow.

Suddenly he saw before him a gap in the mountain, a gap he estimated was not more than half a mile wide.

Part of the lower ground was obscured in cloud, but from his vantage point on the ridge he could see a green, forested valley where in some places there were meadows, and he could make out several lakes. Through the center of the basin, starting not far from where he stood, flowed a small stream.

He climbed down into the basin, going carefully and studying the ground as he went. He had not gone far when he saw a boot print—a small one, and not complete. Only part of the heel showed clearly, but the print appeared to have been made recently.

He went ahead on what seemed to be a game trail, and presently he found a small fir that had been cut partway through with an axe, then broken over to point along the trail. The cut was not new; it appeared to be at least several months old. A short distance farther along a dead branch pointing in the same direction lay across two living branches of a tree.

He came suddenly on the remains of an old campfire, and here again he saw what he thought was the suggestion of a track, scarcely to be made out—not much more than a flattened place at the edge of the campfire.

Brionne studied the site. On a limb nearby hung a pothook made from a forked branch, such as he had often used himself. It showed use; evidently it had been used more than once. This, he felt quite sure, must have been the camp, or one of the camps, that Ed Shaw had used while prospecting in the area.

A small lake was close by, and a spring ran a trickle of water into it. The shore was rocky, but trees came almost to the edge of the water.

Brionne paused inside the belt of trees to consider. The basin was surrounded on three sides by steep mountains, except at the point where he had come through, and undoubtedly at the point where the stream flowed out. The stream rapidly cut more deeply to make a small canyon before it joined the main stream, which was probably Lake Fork Creek.

He returned to the campfire and looked all about. The trail ended here, except for the walk to the edge of the lake for water. Had Shaw, then, entered the lake when he left the camp, and followed along the shore?

Thunder was rumbling now, and there were almost continual flashes of lightning. Here in the forest, with the walls of the ridges closed about him, he felt more secure.

His thoughts returned to the sound he had heard more than once up on the rock ledge. It was unlikely to have been any of the Allards, for there seemed to be none missing except those he himself could account for.

What then? An animal? Some other man? Or perhaps just a dead branch stirred by the wind?

He considered the situation. He could not attack an alerted camp head-on, and such an attack would be to no purpose now. What he wanted was to locate Mat and Miranda. The girl must have known more than she had said, or else she had seen some sign, such as the signs he himself had seen, that had led her closer to finding the mine.

He took a slow circle around the dead campfire, but he found nothing. He tried again, moving farther out, but the result was the same—nothing.

His son was somewhere on this mountain, alone with a young woman who was unfamiliar with the country, and unskilled in its ways. Miranda and Mat had no shelter, no food, no outfit of any kind. Tuley had said that the Allards had that outfit.

A storm was building, a slow, sullen storm that could burst with unbelievable fury at any moment. Moreover, somewhere on this mountain was the Allard gang. And if the Allards found his son they would kill him.

And somewhere on the mountain was Dutton Mowry—a good man, Brionne had believed, but how could he be sure of that now?

Who was Mowry? Why had he come to Promontory? What had led him to take this ride into the mountains with Miranda? Was he, too, after the silver? Did he know something they did not know?

James Brionne sat down on a fallen tree, his shoulders heavy with weariness.

They must be near . . . but where? Could he find them, before the storm struck?

13

The thunder roared upon its great drums, rolling
cataracts of sound down the narrow canyons and
exploding them against the cliffs. Lightning shot in
vivid streaks across the sky, great flashes of light that
seemed not like the lightning seen in the lowlands,
but like a heaven of flame gaping open above them,
giving them a view of the blazing heart of some
other world.

The rain did not come. The atmosphere was
charged with electricity, and the streaks of flame
seemed to bound and rebound from the peaks above
them.

James Brionne got up and walked to the lake

again. A sullen sheet, it lay open to the sky, shining like a great bowl of mercury. He went along the edge, alone in the thickness of cloud that only from time to time tore itself apart and allowed him to peer through, to see the dark firs, the great, craggy rocks, the bleak grayness of the shoreline.

His boy was somewhere not far away, his son who had always been a little frightened of storms—not wishing to admit it, but afraid nonetheless. Was Miranda with him? Something within Brionne assured him that unless torn from Mat's side, she would be there, close beside him. She was that kind of person.

He paused again, during a lull in the cannonade of thunder, to listen for any cry, any call, any human sound at all, but there was none.

He looked about him, shaken with fear for his son, and seemed to see on all sides the evidences of a world in the making—the wind-worn rocks, the long rock-falls of shattered cliffs, the fallen trees, wedged among the rocks and breaking to pieces there, the trails made by rushing water, carrying away the gravel and sand and wearing the rocks as it ran, chafing them, hammering at them with an occasional large rock—everything busy in changing the form of the earth.

These peaks, too, would disappear some day. They would be worn down one day, polished and ancient, their hard-shouldered youth as nothing before the timeless patience of wind and water, of heat and cold, of growth and decay.

A young fir grew from a crack in a boulder where some earth had blown and been held. The roots would split the boulder further apart, and finally the boulder itself would break in half and fall away.

He saw these things, he thought these things, for such thoughts were a part of him. He had been born to see, to observe everything around him. So it was that now he saw something special: a spear of sandstone thrust upright in a crack of the granite—an unnatural thing, surely.

Why was it there? To arrest attention. To catch the eye of the beholder and to let him know that for some reason he must look again. The spear of rock, scarcely two feet long, was canted slightly toward the south. By accident, or design?

He saw that there was a trail, a suggestion of something man-made, a place where there had been movement. Brionne went forward, coming up through the trees to a bald knoll among them, and suddenly from out of the cloud an eagle flew, a lost bird, seeking its nest, confused by the storm, or stunned by the thunder.

The flight of the eagle carried his eye along to the westward, and through the torn clouds he glimpsed the wall of the basin, not far off.

An eagle, one would think, would be safely nested or roosted at such a time. An eagle's instinct would have given him some forewarning of the storm . . . suppose something had disturbed him? Something coming too close to home?

Where had he seen him first? Brionne headed toward where he believed he had first seen the eagle, and when he had walked only a few minutes he came upon the trail again, that suggestion of something man-made.

Then he broke through the last of the firs and saw

the log cabin, built against a shoulder of rock, utilizing the rock for its own rear wall.

Thunder rolled, lightning flared again. How far off was the cabin? Fifty yards? A hundred? He started to run.

And then the rain came.

It came with a burst of fury, whipping, lashing, beating at him; with it came wind and hail. He ran, slowing a little for the uphill slope. He reached the door and pounded on it.

When it did not open, he threw his shoulder against it, and the door gave way. He caught himself just a step inside, and stood there looking into the muzzle of Cotton Allard's gun.

There were four other men with him, one of them the man Brionne had seen in the Southern Hotel in St. Louis, and again in Cheyenne.

At least one other Allard was there. That must be Peabody, of whom he had heard.

Mat was there, too, sitting back in a corner, huddled close to Miranda.

Major James Brionne, his hair plastered against his skull by the rain, water streaming down his face, was soaked to the skin, but he held a rifle in his hand as he stood facing Cotton Allard.

"Drop the rifle," Cotton said. "I got somethin' for you to watch."

The reaction was immediate and swift. James Brionne had learned the zouave drill at St. Cyr, as well as a dozen intricate rifle drills, and now he flipped his rifle forward, spun the butt, and knocked the pistol from Cotton's hand. Then with a butt stroke he smashed one of the other men in the belly, knocking him into a corner.

Peabody lunged at him and Brionne staggered into a corner, falling against the wall. Peabody leaped upon him, but Brionne whipped himself over swiftly and sprang to his feet, even as Cotton scrambled up, gun in hand.

Brionne's gun was in his hand, too, and he looked across the room at Cotton. "You are the gunfighter," he said. "You want to try it with me?"

"Holstered guns?" Cotton suggested, grinning, but it was an evil grin.

"Of course. That is the way, isn't it? One thing, however, let my son and Miss Loften leave the cabin. There is no need for them to get shot by accident."

"Let 'em go," Cotton said. "They ain't goin' no place, and I don't want nothing to happen to that girl yet neither."

Brionne held his gun steady until Mat and Miranda were out of the door. The others trooped out after them.

Rain beat at the walls of the cabin, and on the roof. There was a leak in the corner, another in the center of the roof.

"All right," Cotton said. "We holster our guns, lift our hands, and reach, is that it?"

"Fine." James Brionne was very cool. He had done what he intended to do, and had gotten his son and Miranda outside. He still held his gun.

He was gambling, and he held two cards he was depending on. One of them was his own gun.

"All right," Cotton said, "holster 'em!"

He was superbly confident. In this business of the fast draw, he had seen no one who could equal himself and he was sure this Virginia soldier could not.

Watching carefully for some trick, Brionne drew his gun back, and lowered it carefully to the leather. He had no idea of trying to beat Cotton Allard to the draw. He intended to do just what he was best at. He was going to draw, level his gun, and fire. From the hip, perhaps, if there was no more time, but he was going to aim.

He understood in his cool, careful mind that he was going to get hit. He accepted the fact. But there are many hits that do not kill, and he hoped the shot that hit him would be one of those. On the other hand, he planned to make sure of his own bullet.

Brionne knew that he would probably fire only one shot. He intended that should be enough.

He could hear the pounding rain, he could smell the fire inside the cabin, he could see the savage face of Cotton Allard, the man who had burned his home. Outside was his son, who might die without him if his other gamble did not pay off, or this one.

He felt the muzzle of his gun touch the bottom of the holster, lifted his hand free, and saw that Cotton still gripped his gun.

"So you are a coward, too," he said quietly. "You think you are the best man, but you will not chance it."

Cotton's face flushed with rage. Deliberately, he lifted his hand free; then *"Draw!"* he yelled, and dropped his hand.

Brionne felt his own hand slap the butt, felt the gun start to lift. Cotton's gun was clearing leather, and his face was twisted with triumph and hatred.

"This is for Anne," Brionne said, and for an instant, Cotton's hand froze.

Then his gun leaped up and he fired. Brionne felt the slug as a tremendous blow. It knocked him back through the door. As he tumbled across the threshold he heard the second blast of the gun, and rolled over in the rain and the wet.

He came up to his knees, then to his feet. Something seemed to grip his side, and there was a numbness there. He lifted his gun as Cotton stepped into the door and fired again. Brionne staggered, slipped in trying to regain his balance, and almost fell.

Cotton, his face wolfish, his teeth bared in a kind of snarl, was lifting his gun for another shot. Brionne swung his body around, straightened up, felt the slam of another bullet, but held himself still. He had seen men die, and he had seen too many men take lead to believe that one shot would surely kill, unless by chance or by dead aim. He had no doubt that Cotton could get him, and that he might, but he intended to kill Allard.

He brought his gun down and looked along the barrel at Allard, saw Cotton's eyes blazing with fury, which changed to sudden terror as the gun lined on him. Cotton fired again, and then Brionne squeezed off his shot. He stood in perfect form, firing as if at a target, and he shot Cotton Allard right between the eyes.

Then he turned his gun to Peabody. "You were there," he said, and as Peabody tried to lift his gun, he shot him dead.

"Is there anyone else?" he said calmly.

They stood with their hands up, but they were not looking at him.

He turned and saw Dutton Mowry. The man was using a broken branch for a crutch, and one leg was bandaged and bloody, but he held a six-shooter in one hand. And he was covering them.

"You got here," Brionne said.

"Did you think I wouldn't?" Mowry said.

He gestured to Hoffman and the others. "You boys just shuck your hardware. You'll find a pick and shovel up yonder at the tunnel. Come back down here and bury these men."

James Brionne had not moved. He felt sick and very strange, but he was looking over at Mat, and he wanted to go to him. He willed himself to move, but there was a great weakness in him.

Suddenly Miranda and Mat were running to him. He managed to holster his gun. "I am afraid I shall have to sit down," he said. "I believe I am hit."

They put him down gently at the entrance to the mine and Miranda took off his coat. His shirt was soaked with blood. The bullet had struck his shoulder bone, evidently at an angle, hitting him hard enough to knock him down, and tearing through the muscle at the end of his shoulder.

"He hit me twice, I think. The other one is lower down."

Miranda eased the tail of his shirt from behind his belt, then almost laughed with relief. The bullet had struck his cartridge belt, veered upward and flattened against his money belt, each pocket filled with gold coins.

"You took a chance," she said, "when you didn't throw down your gun."

"We'd have had no chance without it. They were

going to murder us anyway, and I was betting that I could at least kill Cotton, and maybe one other.

"You see, I felt sure Mowry was coming. That was the second gamble I took. It had to be him back there. The more I remembered about him, the more I knew he would not be far behind me."

Mowry was directing Hoffman in building a fire. "You had more confidence than me," he said. "There was a time or two I didn't think I'd make it."

James Brionne leaned back a little, feeling the warmth of the fire and liking it. "I had reason for confidence. Grant never sent a boy to do a man's job."

Dutton Mowry grinned. "Now, how'd you figure that out? Devine told me that if you knew you had a watch dog you'd raise hob."

"General Grant is my friend, and Devine is a worrier. I didn't peg you at first, and then when I had a hunch you took off with Miranda."

Mowry chuckled. "The way I figured it, if you saw me followin' you, with your trouble in Cheyenne, and all, you'd be likely to take a shot at me. Seemed to me that you weren't about to let Miss Loften go off into the mountains without you looking after her. You just ain't that kind of a gent.

"Pat told me you'd been asking about Rody Brennan and Ed Shaw, so I just figured the easiest way to keep account of you was to stay close to Miss Loften here."

Hoffman was puttering with the fire, and now he looked up. He was gaunt and pale. "What are you planning to do with us?"

Brionne glanced at Mowry. "Shall we string them

up? I hear that's the thing to do out here. Or shall we take them down to Brigham's boys? I have a feeling that Porter Rockwell would know just what to do with them."

Hoffman started to protest.

"They've been keeping mighty bad company," Mowry said. "Maybe a long walk might help."

"All right." Brionne sat up, holding his rifle over his knees. "You boys start right off down the trail, and keep going. If we should run into you on the way back—"

"What about our horses?" Miranda protested. "Won't they take them?"

"I found 'em and moved 'em," Mowry said. "I rode one ... that's how I caught up with his nibs here."

When they had gone, Mowry added wood to the fire. "The storm ain't over. I'd best get some fuel."

"You ease that leg," Brionne said. "I'll get it." He got to his feet. He was a little unsteady, but he already felt better. It was all over now.

He walked out in the rain and stood for a moment, just letting the rain fall on him, liking the feel of it. The thunder was sulking in the canyons off to the east; the clouds hung low and heavy over the basin. Standing there in the rain, he felt the tensions of the past few months slowly washing out of him, draining away, and leaving a stillness within him.

He gathered sticks, using only one hand and putting them on the other arm, careful not to hurt the wounded shoulder. He had a bad bruise on his body where the second bullet had smashed against his belts, and that bothered him some. But Mat was all right. He was in there with Miranda, and they were sitting together.

Dutton Mowry eased his leg, and stared out of the door at Brionne. "He's a good man, that one. Take it from a Pinkerton man, who's seen them come and go. He's one of the best."

He glanced around at Miranda. Mat had gone to sleep, his head against her shoulder. "Are you going to grab him?" Mowry asked.

"I'd rather have him than the mine," she said, smiling. "You know, I haven't even thought about it since we got here. I don't know whether there's anything up there or not. And do you know something else? I don't really care."

James Brionne was coming back into the cabin as she spoke. He was carrying an armful of branches he had broken from a deadfall. He dropped the wood just inside the door.

"I think the rain is easing up," he said. "I'll go get the horses."

ABOUT THE AUTHOR

Louis L'Amour, born Louis Dearborn L'Amour, is of French-Irish descent. Although Mr. L'Amour claims his writing began as a "spur-of-the-moment thing," prompted by friends who relished his verbal tales of the West, he comes by his talent honestly. A frontiersman by heritage (his grandfather was scalped by the Sioux), and a universal man by experience, Louis L'Amour lives the life of his fictional heroes. Since leaving his native Jamestown, North Dakota, at the age of fifteen, he's been a longshoreman, lumberjack, elephant handler, hay shocker, flume builder, fruit picker, and an officer on tank destroyers during World War II. And he's written four hundred short stories and over fifty books (including a volume of poetry).

Mr. L'Amour has lectured widely, traveled the West thoroughly, studied archaeology, compiled biographies of over one thousand Western gunfighters, and read prodigiously (his library holds more than two thousand volumes). And he's watched thirty-one of his westerns as movies. He's circled the world on a freighter, mined in the West, sailed a dhow on the Red Sea, been shipwrecked in the West Indies, stranded in the Mojave Desert. He's won fifty-one of fifty-nine fights as a professional boxer and pinch-hit for Dorothy Kilgallen when she was on vacation from her column. Since 1816, thirty-three members of his family have been writers. And, he says, "I could sit in the middle of Sunset Boulevard and write with my typewriter on my knees; temperamental I am not."

Mr. L'Amour is re-creating an 1865 Western town, christened Shalako, where the borders of Utah, Arizona, New Mexico, and Colorado meet. Historically authentic from whistle to well, it will be a live, operating town, as well as a movie location and tourist attraction.

Mr. L'Amour now lives in Los Angeles with his wife Kathy, who helps with the enormous amount of research he does for his books. Soon, Mr. L'Amour hopes, the children (Beau and Angelique) will be helping too.

BANTAM'S #1
ALL-TIME BESTSELLING AUTHOR
AMERICA'S FAVORITE WESTERN WRITER

☐	24100	HELLER WITH A GUN	$2.50
☐	23368	BOWDRIE	$2.95
☐	23233	CROSS FIRE TRAIL	$2.50
☐	23143	SHOWDOWN AT YELLOW BUTTE	$2.50
☐	23263	CHANCY	$2.50
☐	24289	SITKA	$2.95
☐	20846	THE CHEROKEE TRAIL	$2.95
☐	23219	MOUNTAIN VALLEY WAR	$2.50
☐	22799	TAGGART	$2.50
☐	23153	HIGH LONESOME	$2.50
☐	22814	BORDEN CHANTRY	$2.50
☐	20880	BRIONNE	$2.50
☐	20883	THE FERGUSON RIFLE	$2.50
☐	20882	KILLOE	$2.50
☐	22843	CONAGHER	$2.50
☐	23448	NORTH TO THE RAILS	$2.50
☐	23262	THE MAN FROM SKIBBEREEN	$2.50
☐	23010	SILVER CANYON	$2.50
☐	22901	CATLOW	$2.50
☐	22985	GUNS OF THE TIMBERLANDS	$2.50
☐	14042	HANGING WOMAN CREEK	$2.50
☐	22636	FALLON	$2.50
☐	23222	UNDER THE SWEETWATER RIM	$2.50
☐	22983	MATAGORDA	$2.50
☐	22639	DARK CANYON	$2.50
☐	20956	THE CALIFORNIOS	$2.50

Prices and availability subject to change without notice.